Not-so-sweet sixteen

"So you didn't tell me your parents were throwing you a major sweet-sixteen party!" Liza exclaimed. "Gavin told me all about it. It sounds awesome! Everyone from your class—cool Californians, Dylan . . ."

"Uh, Liza," Laurel said, beginning to sweat. "Um . . ." She had to tell Liza she'd made up all that so Gavin wouldn't think she was pining away for him. Liza would understand. But suddenly she couldn't bear to speak the truth. That there was no party. That her parents were too busy to even remember her birthday. That she couldn't bear to see Gavin and pretend everything was okay. That she'd misread everything that had happened with Dylan tonight.

You have to tell Liza the truth, Laurel thought. *She's your best friend. If you can't be a total lameoid with your best friend, then who can you be one with?*

"Liza, um, there's—"

"Uh-oh, gotta go," Liza interrupted. "My mom's coming. I'll call you tomorrow!"

Click. Laurel sighed and clicked off herself. She slumped over her desk; her head felt like it weighed a hundred pounds.

She'd tell Liza the truth tomorrow. For tonight, just tonight, she actually wanted to *believe* she was having that amazing sweet sixteen. With doting parents, new friends, and a cute, new adoring guy.

Just for tonight. Even if Dylan wouldn't be her date in a million years.

Super Edition

Sweet Sixteen

ALLISON RAINE

BANTAM BOOKS
NEW YORK · TORONTO · LONDON · SYDNEY · AUCKLAND

RL: 6, AGES 012 AND UP

SWEET SIXTEEN
A Bantam Book / August 2000

Cover photography by Michael Segal.

Produced by 17th Street Productions,
an Alloy Online, Inc. company.
33 West 17th Street
New York, NY 10011.

ISBN: 0-553-49325-6

Visit us on the Web! www.randomhouse.com/teens

Published simultaneously in the United States and Canada

PRINTED IN THE UNITED STATES OF AMERICA

OPM   0 9 8 7 6 5 4 3 2 1

To Mom and Dad,
who've been ardent supporters of my writing
since the days of the broken pretzels.

One

LAUREL BAYER WAS beyond miserable. Come to think of it, *miserable* wasn't even the word to describe how she was feeling. Beyond *heartbroken* was more like it.

Add to that a new school, no friends for thousands of miles, and a too-busy-to-notice family. *Just what every girl wants for her sixteenth birthday,* Laurel thought as she flung herself onto her bed.

Your birthday isn't for two weeks, she reminded herself. *Your whole life could change in fourteen days.*

Eleven days, to be exact.

Yeah. And maybe if she blinked twice, she'd be back in her hometown of Grange, Ohio, living across the street from her two best friends, walking hand in hand with Gavin—

Laurel blinked twice, just in case. Nope. Nothing. She was still lying on her back on the

1

middle of her brand-new bed in the middle of her brand-new bedroom in the middle of brand-new-to-her Pasadena, California.

She sat up, hugging her legs to her chest and grabbing Harold, the ratty stuffed brown bear she'd had since she was two years old. She ran a finger over Harold's pink-threaded nose.

Don't look, she told herself as the tears threatened. *Don't look.* But she couldn't help it. Straight ahead, atop her brand-new oak dresser, the major source of her misery smiled up at her.

Gavin.

Well, a photograph of Gavin. He stood between Laurel and their mutual best friend, Liza. He had an arm around each of them, and he was laughing at a joke Laurel had told them. Laurel's mom had snapped the photo just a few days before the Bayers moved from Ohio to California. Before . . .

Before Laurel had idiotically told Gavin—after ten years of platonic best friendship—that she liked him more than as a friend. Liked him . . . a lot. That she loved him, *that* way. His response? A sudden, awkward stuttering attack, followed by, "Uh . . . I love you too, Laurel. Just not like . . . *that.*"

Tears pricked Laurel's eyes at the memory. She jumped up and flipped the photo over, unable to look at Gavin's amazing dark blue eyes any longer. Then she fell back on the bed and hugged Harold to her stomach. Had it been only two weeks ago that Laurel had gone for a walk with Gavin and uttered those fateful words: *There's something I have to tell you before I go . . . ?*

And had it been only two weeks ago that she, Gavin, and Liza had said good-bye in front of the Bayers' house in Ohio? Two weeks since she'd told Gavin everything between them was fine, not to worry, they were still best buds? Two weeks since Gavin had been so awkward about kissing her on the cheek before she and her folks drove off to the airport?

She'd comforted *him*. Assured *him* that *she* was fine. Assured *him* that *she'd* get over it. After all, she was moving to sunny California, right? Land of bright sunshine and megawatt smiles. They were still the best of friends, right? And the distance—or what she'd confessed—wouldn't change that, right?

Right. Right. Right.

Ha.

Laurel heard a car honk and instinctively ran to the window as though Gavin or Liza would be waiting for her outside. "We're not in Ohio anymore, Harold," she whispered. A tanned blonde with golden hair and golden legs hopped into a red convertible, kissed the cute, sunglasses-wearing driver, and off they went.

Talk about a total southern-California cliché.

Laurel moved to the large, oval mirror that hung above her dresser. She took in her reflection, trying to imagine what someone meeting her for the first time would see. An athletic, five-foot-three frame. Thick, dark brown, straight, shoulder-length hair. Very big, very round, dark brown eyes. Slightly olive complexion. Oh yeah, your typical California girl—a dead ringer for Rebecca Romijn-Stamos.

The phone rang, and Laurel's heart leaped. *Please be Gavin,* she thought desperately, *telling me how much you miss me. That you realized you love me too. That somehow we'll work out a long-distance relationship.* She snatched the cordless off her desk. "Hello?"

"Nervous about the first day of school tomorrow?"

Laurel dropped back down onto her bed, instantly comforted by her best friend's voice. To go from talking to Liza multiple times a day to once or twice a week had been tough to get used to. "Beyond nervous."

"So what are you gonna wear?" Liza asked. "I say go for the minisundress I gave you or the black capris with the pale pink cardigan over the shell. Ooh, or maybe jeans and your new Steve Madden sandals so you don't look like you're trying—"

Laurel laughed. Liza was a clotheshorse, and sometimes she forgot that Laurel was the opposite. "I'll figure out something. I still can't believe I'm starting my junior year of high school without you."

"I know. Me either."

"Do you think private school is going to be really different?" Laurel had won an academic scholarship to The Hunt School. During a house-hunting trip two months ago, she and her parents had visited Hunt for a tour and to meet the principal. Private, small, and very la-di-da, Hunt was nothing like her old high school.

"Nah," Liza assured her. "It's all the same stuff—guys, popularity, classes. Don't worry. Hey, this is so weird. I can't even tell you face-to-face about the hot guy I met at the mall last night!"

"Gimme the details," Laurel said with a laugh. Liza was a guy *magnet*. Unlike Laurel. Her friend had already had countless boyfriends, while Laurel had had a big, whopping zero. *Probably because I always measured every guy against Gavin . . .*

"He's really cute," Liza gushed. "His name's Brian. We're going out tomorrow night."

"That's great, Liza."

"I'm such a dork!" Liza replied. "I can't believe I'm going on and on about some guy when I know you're probably thinking about Gavin. I'll bet you're twirling your hair around your finger like you always do when you're upset or nervous, right?"

"I am not," Laurel protested, releasing her finger from her hair. Tears filling her eyes, she gripped the phone as though it were a lifeline. She'd twirled her hair nonstop the night her feelings for Gavin

5

had suddenly changed. She and her sister Dani had gotten into another stupid fight over nothing, and Laurel had run over to Gavin's—as usual—to vent. Something in the way he'd hugged her in comfort—despite the fact that he'd hugged her a million times before—had awakened something inside her. She'd been so aware of him as a *guy* instead of just regular old Gavin. And she'd felt different too . . . like a *girl* instead of regular old Laurel.

Liza had recommended that Laurel tell Gavin how she felt. But Laurel couldn't. It was never the right moment. Week. Month. Until the day before Laurel was moving halfway across the world from him. *Idiot.*

"Have you heard from him?" Liza asked.

Laurel squeezed her eyes shut. "Just a few e-mails to ask how the flight went and to say hi. Nothing about . . . us."

"I'm sorry, Laur." Liza sighed. "But at least you tried. Even if it didn't work out like you hoped, at least you finally told him how you felt."

"I guess," Laurel choked out, fighting back tears. "He hasn't talked about it with you?"

"No," Liza said. "And I doubt he'll bring it up. He knows that's between you and him. He probably doesn't even think I know about it."

"Maybe," Laurel managed.

"Hey, c'mon," Liza said. "I'll bet in a month you and Gavin will be the same old buds, e-mailing every five minutes with every mundane thing that happens. Just give it a couple more weeks to settle down, okay?"

Laurel knew Liza was right. But that didn't make it hurt any less.

"I wish we could fly out for your birthday," Liza said.

The thought didn't make Laurel feel better. Two weeks ago the idea of her two best friends flying out for her sixteenth birthday would have had her jumping for joy. Now . . . how could she face Gavin again as if everything was all right when it wasn't?

"Me too," Laurel half lied. She did wish *Liza* could fly out to California.

"Even if we could come, you probably wouldn't have time for us," Liza said. "You're gonna make so many new friends at Hunt that your sweet sixteen will be mobbed with people. You won't even notice that your boring old midwestern friends are there."

As if I'm having *a sweet-sixteen party,* Laurel thought, gnawing her lower lip. Her parents were so wrapped up in the move and preparing for their new jobs that they probably didn't even remember her birthday was coming up. Plus Laurel didn't know a soul in California, and she doubted she'd make friends right away. Who would she invite even if she *did* have a party? Her parents? Her two sisters, who were away at college?

She'd always thought she'd have a sweet-sixteen party. Not one of those killer functions at a country club, but a fun party at her house with her friends and tons of M&M's and good music. Now she'd be lucky if anyone said "happy birthday" to her.

"I'd better go before my dad keels over about the phone bills we're gonna run up," Liza told Laurel. "We'd better try to stick to e-mail. And hey—good luck tomorrow!"

"Thanks, Liza," Laurel whispered, her voice catching. "Bye."

As Laurel put the phone down on her desk, her computer seemed to be challenging her: *Turn me on, check me for e-mail from Gavin—again,* the iMac seemed to be taunting. *Like there'll be any. Ha, ha, ha!*

Whoa. There it was. New mail from Gavin!

Laurel took a deep breath and clicked open the message.

> *Hey, Laur: How's California and the beach and all? Everything's the same here, except you're (unfortunately) really far away. I'm glad everything's okay between us. I've always been able to tell you everything, and if I had to keep this new news a secret from you, I'd hate that! Guess who I hooked up with last night? Geena Moore! I know you and Liza think she's Ms. Stuck-up Cheerleader, but she's not like that. Geena and I talked for, like, hours last night. Okay, okay, we*

*made out too. It's so weird, Laur—I can't
remember ever feeling like this about a girl
before, and—*

Laurel couldn't read another word.

How *could* he? How could he be so insensitive?
So thoughtless? How could he pretend she hadn't
told him she loved him? And *Geena Moore?* That
was the kind of girl Gavin wanted? A big-haired
airhead with big boobs?

How could he be so mean? Yeah, she'd told him
everything was okay between them, but he hadn't
really believed her, had he?

Apparently he had.

Welcome to the land of sunshine and smiles.

"Junior year is gonna be so great!"

Dylan Fraiser held the phone farther away from
his ear. His best friend, Dave Cranston, was a little
too psyched for school to start tomorrow.

Dylan couldn't be *less* psyched. He'd do anything to be back with his mom in Tel Aviv, Israel,
where he'd spent the summer. He'd met the most
interesting people, seen amazing things, and heard
about issues he'd never even *thought* to think about
before. And now here he was, holed up with his
dad, who talked about only one thing: Dylan's
grades.

Nothing interesting ever happened in Pasadena.
And no one but Dylan seemed to care.

"We're juniors!" Dave yelled. "We're finally up-perclassmen. How cool is that, man!"

Dylan ran a hand through his thick, blond hair and blew out a sigh. "Oh, really cool. Now we'll get the usual boredom and the added bonus of stressing over taking the SATs."

"Man, oh, man," Dave said. "Lighten up."

"Okay, give me one good reason why I want to walk into Hunt tomorrow morning." As Dylan let Dave rack his brain for an answer, he reached for the varnished walking stick propped up against the wall behind his bed. His mom had sent it to him from Africa last year. He wrapped his hand around the shiny, dark wood. If only Dylan could live with his mom for longer than just a summer and travel with her wherever her UN job took her. His life would be so much better.

"Okay, how about the soccer team?" Dave said. "Or the debate team? Or your art classes."

Try again, buddy, Dylan thought. "I could join a soccer league in town, argue with you for hours, and paint on the beach."

"Okay . . . how about this," Dave said. "Since you're a junior now, not to mention bizarrely pop-ular *despite* your bad attitude, you've now got the freshman and sophomore chicks idolizing you like you're Chris Klein or something. Plus you can have your pick of girls in our class. And you're not too young anymore for the senior babes. You can have *any* girl you want . . . well, except for the ones

10

you already hooked up with and dissed. Oh, wait a minute, that's practically *all* of them."

As Dave dissolved into laughter, Dylan leaned the stick carefully back against the wall. "Very funny," he barked into the receiver as he stared out the window at the moonless night sky. Okay, so he *had* fooled around with a lot of girls from Hunt. But he hadn't dissed them; he just hadn't been interested in a relationship. "Most Hunt girls are the same," Dylan complained. "Boring and superficial."

Dave coughed. "You really want to spend your Saturday nights debating Mideast peace issues with some girl?"

Dylan stared up at the stars. "I'm just saying I want more than the usual stupid conversations about nothing. Cafeteria food, what someone else said, boring gossip, who fooled around with who, where some girl's having her stupid sweet-sixteen party. Man, who *cares?* The girls I met in Israel had so much going on—more than having to choose DJs and menus for birthday parties. I mean, they have to go into the *army*. Can you imagine that?"

"I don't think I *want* to imagine a girl with a machine gun."

Dylan laughed; he couldn't help it. "Look, you're missing my point—"

"Hey, bud, I hear you loud and clear," Dave interrupted. "But here's why you're wrong. Not

11

every girl at Hunt is a boring airhead. The hot ones *you* go for, okay, maybe most of them are fluff brains. So blame that on your own superficial taste. But there are many exceptions. My own very pretty girlfriend is the farthest thing from boring and superficial."

"I didn't mean Ca—"

"I know, I know," Dave said. "I'm just giving you the hard time you deserve. Not every guy can be as lucky as me and have Cara for a girlfriend. Smart *and* gorgeous."

"What she sees in a loser like you . . . ," Dylan said with a laugh. Cara *was* a great girl—perfect for Dave. Dylan had always been a little jealous of what they had; their connection was deep and real. Most people thought Dylan was a commitmentphobe because of his parents' bitter divorce. But it wasn't the divorce that made him shun relationships with the girls he hooked up with. It was the girls themselves.

If Dylan could meet a girl who made him feel the way Cara made Dave feel, he'd be Mr. Boyfriend in a second.

But he'd never find that girl at The Hunt School.

Never.

TWO

LAUREL JUMPED OUT of bed the next morning before her alarm clock buzzed, even though last night had been one of the worst *ever*. She'd dreamed about Gavin. Pathetic dreams. Gavin, standing in the great field by her old house, his arms opened wide, calling out her name. Laurel, running toward him across the flat expanse of dandelions. But just as Laurel reached him, Geena Moore, with her dyed blond hair and Wonderbra–enhanced chest, would push her out of the way. Gavin would whisper a shrugged "sorry" to Laurel, leaving her crying on the ground while he and Geena skipped away. . . .

Go take a very hot shower, she ordered herself. *And forget about Gavin. You don't want to walk into the world of Baywatch High looking all upset and intense. This is California!*

13

Laurel headed down the hall to the bathroom. Her parents' bedroom door was closed, and she didn't hear a sound. The whole house was silent. Her parents couldn't be still asleep, could they? Maybe they'd already left for their jobs? She knew The Hunt School was only a ten-minute walk, but she'd sort of expected one of her parents to drive her the first day. For luck. Well, more like for *comfort*.

By the stairs, Laurel trained her ear for kitchen sounds. Nothing. Dead quiet. *Yeah, like my parents are really going to think about throwing me a sweet-sixteen party,* Laurel thought. *They can't even remember I exist!*

One hot shower later, Laurel felt a little better— but a lot more nervous about her first day at her new school. *What did Liza tell me to wear?* she wondered as she towel dried her hair on the way back to her bedroom. *The sundress? Jeans?*

She opened her closet and stared at her uninspired wardrobe. She fingered the blue sundress for a moment. She'd feel too dressed up. Back in Ohio, everyone just wore jeans to school. She pulled her favorite jeans off a hanger, then reached for her gray V-necked baby tee from a shelf. She wouldn't call attention to herself, and she'd be comfortable. Perfect.

Once she was dressed, Laurel combed her hair, applied a little clear lip gloss, and grabbed her navy blue backpack, which she'd packed last night with the usual school items. Notebooks. Pens. Pencils. Tissues. Wallet. Date book. She made sure she had her gym stuff for soccer tryouts, which were being held after school. Sneakers, shorts, T-shirt, socks. Scrunchie. She was ready.

Not quite. There was one thing she had to do before leaving. Respond to Gavin's e-mail.

Laurel sat down at her desk and typed back:

> Gavin—
> Of course everything's okay between us! And congrats about Geena. If you like her, she's gotta be nicer than Liza and I thought. Things are going great here. My parents are planning my sweet-sixteen party, and I get to invite the entire junior class at my new school! Hunt's a lot smaller than District, so everyone's really tight. At least that's what the guy I met on the beach yesterday told me. He's taking me out tonight to celebrate my first day at Hunt. People here are so nice! Well, gotta get to school!
>
> —Laurel

Laurel reread her message. It sounded perfect. Except for the fact that everything she'd said was a total lie. She was about to delete the entire thing and just type back a *hi, things are fine, congrats about Geena,* but she couldn't.

Is it really so wrong to want him to think I'm over him

15

and having a blast? Laurel wondered. *After that e-mail he sent me? Besides, everything I wrote has the potential to come true, right?*

She *could* possibly have a party. She *could* possibly invite everyone at Hunt. She *could* possibly meet a guy on the beach. He *could* possibly ask her out. . . .

And it wasn't like Gavin would ever know otherwise.

Just hit the send button, Laurel ordered herself. It *was* the right response to his e-mail, as though they were the same old best friends they'd always been, as though she hadn't opened her heart to him.

As though he hadn't broken it in two.

Laurel hit send.

She took a deep breath, shouldered her backpack, and then froze at the sight of the photo of her, Liza, and Gavin. Laurel picked up the heavy frame, opened her top dresser drawer, and tucked it inside.

She headed downstairs. The smell of the freshly painted walls overwhelmed her. *Everything* was new in this house. Out of habit, Laurel turned left at the bottom of the stairs but found herself face-to-face with the door to the basement. Laurel squeezed her eyes shut, counted to five, and turned around. *You'll figure out this house soon enough,* she told herself. *You'll figure out this town. You'll figure out the shortest way to school. Don't worry. You're gonna be sixteen in two weeks. You're not a kid anymore.*

Laurel turned around and walked into the kitchen. She opened four cabinets before she found the bowls and two drawers before she found a spoon. After two weeks of living in this house, she still couldn't find anything! Luckily she couldn't miss the refrigerator. One bowl of Special K later, Laurel tried to ignore the butterflies that were beginning to flutter around in her stomach.

"Ready for your first day?"

Laurel whipped around, never so happy to see her dad. "I thought you and Mom were both gone already."

Don Bayer straightened his tie, then leaned down to give Laurel a kiss on the forehead. "Well, Mom left about an hour ago. She's got that crazy commute. But she gave me special instructions to give you a kiss and wish you luck on your first day of school. So how about a kiss and hug for your dad? It's my first day of school too."

Laurel smiled and threw her arms around her father. Weird. No matter how old she got, nothing ever felt better than a bear hug from her dad. "I *wish* we could trade places. I'll be the dean of faculty at Caltech, and *you* can be the new kid at Hunt."

Her dad laughed. "You know, it's a 'first day' for all of us. Your mom at her new job at the

Web site. Mine at Caltech. And your sisters too. Dani's first day of classes as a freshman at Ohio State, and Julie begins her third year of med school."

Laurel hadn't really thought of it that way. *All* the Bayers were starting something new. Her dad's new position at Caltech was the reason they'd moved in the first place. Maybe she *had* been a little preoccupied with herself.

"Ready, hon?" her dad asked, fishing his keys out of his pocket.

"Ready," Laurel said, taking a deep breath.

Once they were settled in her dad's ancient blue Volvo and headed on their way, Laurel's dad squeezed her hand. "Your mom and I are both so proud of you, Laur. You're handling this move really well. We know it wasn't easy leaving your friends."

Friend, Laurel corrected mentally. Only Liza. She wasn't quite sure how to classify Gavin now. Would a friend have really sent her that e-mail? *Stop thinking about Gavin,* she ordered herself. *You're on your way to a new life!* "Thanks, Dad." She wondered if she should remind him about her birthday, ask if he and her mom were planning something. But her dad seemed kind of nervous. This probably wasn't the right time.

A thousand butterflies let loose in Laurel's stomach as the quaint, pretty buildings of Hunt came into view. As they passed the white gate with

18

its green-and-white The Hunt School sign, Laurel thought she might throw up.

Calm down, she told herself. *It's just a school. It's filled with people, like back in Ohio. No biggie.*

Her dad pulled to a stop in front of the main entrance. The Hunt School was made up of several brick houses, joined by beautifully manicured courtyards. Laurel's new classmates were milling around, running into different buildings, and hugging each other in greeting. With their trendy outfits and perfect hair, they all looked like extras on *Dawson's Creek.* *Or models in a Delia's catalog.* Laurel bit her lip.

"Jen! How was Paris?"

Laurel watched two girls kiss one cheek, then the other. Well, kiss the air, actually. The question asker wore a skimpy, clingy, black tank dress and at least three-inch heels. Jen wore an outfit Laurel imagined you'd find in *Vogue.*

Paris? Laurel thought, glancing down at her lap. This T-shirt and jeans might be the cool uniform back home, but suddenly Laurel felt completely *un-*cool. And the thought of stepping out of this car and into that crowd made Laurel's stomach turn over and her knees feel like jelly.

"Have a great day, sweetheart," her dad said.

Laurel swallowed.

So predictable, Dylan thought, watching Sophie Hernandez and Melissa Hollis, two juniors, screech

19

and hug as he neared his homeroom. It was always the same on the first day of school. Totally phony.

"I love your sandals," Melissa gushed to Sophie. "Omigod, are those Prada?"

"I got them in Italy," Sophie said. "Early birthday present from my stepmother."

"Hey, are you having your sweet sixteen at Lux's?" Ashlina Jones asked Sophie. "I'm thinking of having mine there, but Daddy says they'll be booked for corporate Christmas parties in December."

Can I barf now at how pretentious you girls are? Dylan thought in disgust.

"Hey, Dylan," Sophie called out, twirling her silver-chain necklace around her finger.

Dylan shot her a reasonably friendly smile and headed inside. These girls were supposed to make him excited about another school year? Dave had it all wrong.

"Hey, Fraiser."

"Dylan."

"How's it going?"

"Hi, Dylan."

"Dylan, hi!"

"Hi, Dylan . . ."

Dylan high-fived his friends, a couple of guys from the soccer team, one from debate, and a few who knew him from classes, and he smiled friendly smiles at the girls. Then he headed toward the back of the room and dropped down in a seat, hoping to catch a prehomeroom nap. He'd tossed and turned all night long. Thinking about some of the stuff Dave had said, maybe. He *wasn't* a user. No way. He'd never intentionally hurt anyone.

"Hi, Dylan."

How many fake smiles am I going to have to plaster on my face before this day is done? Dylan wondered. He glanced up to see Amanda Lang standing before him. Shifting in his seat, Dylan ran a hand through his hair, forcing the smile. The last time he'd seen Amanda was in June, at Tim Hong's party, when he'd . . . well, hooked up with her.

Your own fault, Dylan reminded himself, swallowing as Amanda beamed at him. Amanda was pretty and sweet, but she talked nonstop about suntan lotions and which beaches were her favorites. At the party he'd tried to talk to her about creative writing since she was on the literary magazine's staff, but she'd told him she only joined to enhance her college applications.

I will never again fool around with a girl just because she's attractive, Dylan promised himself. It was stupid. And immature. Just once he wanted to hear a girl talk passionately about a subject other than her appearance—or appearanc*es*.

Mr. Harris, the homeroom teacher, walked into the room and called the class to order. Amanda's eyes darted in Mr. Harris's direction, then back to Dylan. "Talk to you later," she whispered seductively.

21

Dylan nodded, silently thanking Mr. Harris for his good timing.

"Welcome back," the teacher said. "Okay, first we've got some scheduling changes. Painting II has been moved to periods four and five, Mondays and Thursdays. . . ."

What? Dylan thought. *They rescheduled Painting II?* He opened his backpack, searching around for his schedule. Painting II was the one class Dylan was really looking forward to. If he had to drop it because—

"Who cares about painting?" Ashlina whispered to the girl sitting next to her. "Like anyone interested in the Ivy League would waste credits on arts and crafts."

Dylan rolled his eyes. *He* cared about painting. He unfolded his schedule and scanned it. Oh, man! Period four on Monday and Thursday was when he had debate-club sessions. If it were up to Dylan, he'd drop debate for painting in a second. But his dad would never stand for it, for the very reason Ashlina had just stated.

Dylan let out a heavy sigh. There was no use in even bringing this up with his father; Stephen Fraiser couldn't care less if Dylan painted or not. What made Dylan feel truly happy was irrelevant to him. All he cared about was Dylan's GPA. And his *intellectual* extracurriculars. He stared at his schedule, trying to see if there was any way he could shuffle everything around. Maybe he could. . . . But that would require moving physics to his English slot, and then who knew when he'd be able to fit in history. . . .

Frustrated, Dylan crumpled up the piece of paper, leaning back against the wall.

Man. When was this year going to be over?

"Daddy said I can't go over ten thousand dollars for my sweet sixteen. Hel-lo! Like I'm supposed to have some substandard band? I might even have to settle for a DJ!"

"My stepmother's taking me shopping to Beverly Hills for my dress."

"Do you think I can book the country club for next month?"

"I heard Ava invited the whole class to her party."

"Omigod—everyone's gonna go. I'm totally jealous of where she's having hers."

"I heard that Sally Peidmont's is at a chain restaurant off the freeway. Can you believe that?"

"Omigod, guys, that's so mean. Her parents must be really poor."

"I'm so glad it's almost the end of the year. I've bought, like, eight hundred sweet-sixteen presents already!"

"Welcome back, class!"

Laurel sat frozen in her homeroom seat, still too afraid to raise her eyes from her desk now that the teacher had arrived. Ten-thousand-dollar budgets? Beverly Hills for dresses? Omigod?

Laurel hadn't known that anyone actually said *omigod* for real.

How was she going to fit in?

As Ms. Lopez introduced herself, took roll call, and discussed the off-campus-privileges policy, Laurel finally took the opportunity to glance around the room. Hunt was radically different from District High. For one, there were five hundred students instead of two thousand. Ten per homeroom instead of thirty. And unlike the large, sterile classrooms with fluorescent lighting at District, this room was cozy and unique, with arched windows and wooden carvings on the walls. The only familiar thing was the metal chairs/desks.

Laurel's gaze stopped on a girl sitting by the door. Ava Landau, she'd learned from roll call. The one who'd supposedly invited the entire class to her sweet sixteen. Laurel wondered when the party was. Would she be the only person in the junior class who wasn't there? Ava was beautiful and stylish, with long, light brown hair and blue eyes. The white cotton pants and white tank top on her model-like frame looked so perfect. *On me, that would look like pj's,* Laurel thought. She'd noticed Ava before homeroom, surrounded by three cute guys in the hallway. Granted, Ava wasn't blond, but she was Miss California regardless.

Laurel almost couldn't bear to look at Ava anymore. She shifted her gaze around the room, feeling horribly lonely. Was there anyone here she would actually be friends with? Or would she be playing the part of the new girl all year long?

You're gonna make so many new friends to invite to your sweet-sixteen party that you won't even notice your boring old midwestern friends. . . .

She wondered what the gossipy girls would think if they knew any sweet sixteen Laurel would have would probably be in her parents' backyard and involve a grill and a radio.

The bell rang, startling Laurel out of her worries.

"Class," Ms. Lopez called above the noise of students getting up, gathering their stuff, and talking. "We had so much to cover this morning that I wasn't able to properly introduce our new student! Class, please welcome Laurel Bayer to Hunt. She's from Ohio." Laurel felt her earlobes burn as all eyes swung to her. She managed a weak smile. Everyone probably thought Ohio was the boonies.

"It sucks to be new, huh?"

Laurel glanced up to find a pretty, petite girl with shiny, chin-length hair smiling at her. She smiled back. "Definitely."

"I'm Cara Kwei. The principal assigned me as your orientation 'buddy' since we have the same schedule. Sorry I didn't say hi before homeroom started, but I got here too late. I know what it's like to be new since I moved here as a freshman," Cara chatted on as she led the way out. "Don't worry about a thing. Hunt's a small school, and people are really friendly. I mean, there are cliques, but every school has that."

Laurel nodded. Cara seemed really nice. *And* she was wearing jeans and a T-shirt, just like Laurel.

Cara rolled her eyes as three girls with the same hairstyle (model straight with a slight flip at the ends), the same outfit (tight black pants and a black tank top), and the same lipstick (a matte brownish red) walked by. "And of course, we also have our share of clones," she added.

Laurel grinned.

Well. Maybe she would have a friend here after all.

Three

Lunch tray in hand, Dylan was trying to think of ways to graduate early as he scanned the cafeteria for Dave and Cara.

"Hi, Dylan!"

"Hi, Dylan!"

"*Hi*, Dylan . . ."

On and on the *hi, Dylans* went, from groups of pretty girls. Dylan said his hellos back and sighed inwardly. Why *was* he so popular with girls anyway? He wasn't exactly the friendliest guy in the world, and he *did* sort of have a bad attitude. Was it because he'd been voted—embarrassingly enough—Best Looking both freshman and sophomore year? *So girls like the way I look,* he thought. *Is that all they really care about? I mean, does Amanda want to hook up again only because she thinks I'm good-looking?*

I'll bet she'd stare at me blankly if I tried talking to her about my parents' divorce or about the rules of soccer.

Dylan shook his head and headed for the open doors that led out to the patio. Ah. There they were. Dave and Cara sat at a small, round table with some girl Dylan didn't recognize. The brunette didn't look like the typical Hunt girlie girl. She was laughing at something Dave had said, a real, genuine belly laugh instead of the usual breathy giggle. Plus she was wearing a gray T-shirt and jeans.

"Hey, guys," he said, dropping down in the empty seat next to Cara—and across from the mystery girl.

"Dylan!" Cara exclaimed, reaching over to give him a kiss on the cheek. "We were just talking about you."

Dylan raised an eyebrow.

"Meet Laurel Bayer," Cara said. "She's new. From Ohio. Laurel, this is Dylan Fraiser."

Laurel. What a cool name. "Hi." Ohio, huh? He'd never met anyone from Ohio. Maybe she wasn't the typical California golden girl with sand for brains.

"Hi." Laurel smiled at him.

"She was on her soccer team at her old high school," Dave added, popping a waffle french fry into his mouth.

Dylan took a sip of his orange juice. So she was an athlete. And a soccer player, *his* sport. Interesting.

"Which is why you came up," Cara added.

Laurel took a sip of her soda. "They tell me you're an amazing goalie."

Dylan tried to shrug off the compliment by taking a bite of his turkey sandwich, but he was secretly pleased. "My friends tend to exaggerate."

"Dylan's the best player Hunt's ever seen." Dave smirked at Dylan. "Then again, we *are* talking about a wimp sport. If we were discussing football, however—"

"Wimp sport?" Laurel interjected, her eyes widening. "*Soccer* takes more technique, agility, and skill than any other team sport. That's why it's the most popular spectator sport in the world—except for the United States."

Dave held up his hands in surrender. "Whoa, touchy. You soccer types are all the same."

Dylan laughed and looked at Laurel. She had a really sexy dimple. And the biggest eyes he'd ever seen. "He's *always* on me about soccer. I'm glad to have someone on my side."

Laurel grinned and popped a french fry into her mouth. Dylan noticed the girl was actually eating real food: a hamburger and fries. Most girls Dylan knew wouldn't touch something that might contain fat, let alone red meat.

Out of the corner of his eye Dylan noticed that Cara was giving him a look. A look that said, *Don't you dare even think about using and abusing this new girl.*

Cara wouldn't warn Laurel about his, um, track record with girls, would she? He wouldn't even get the chance to find out if she was as interesting as she seemed.

"So what's your next class?" Dylan asked Laurel. "I've got poetry."

"Us too," Cara answered quickly, narrowing her eyes at Dylan. "Laurel and I have the same schedule. I'm her orientation buddy. In fact, I've been telling her *everything* I think a new girl should know about Hunt. Of course, I'm not *finished* yet."

Dylan raised an eyebrow. Great. She'd never let him near Laurel!

Laurel. What kind of name is that? Dylan wondered as he watched the soccer tryouts from the bleachers. *I wonder why she moved from Ohio. What's Ohio even* like?

"Hey, Fraiser. You have any thoughts on Griffin?" Coach Diego asked as he sat down next to Dylan, his eyes on the field.

Dylan focused on the redheaded junior that Coach was referring to. At the moment Griffin was waiting in line to do some soccer drills. "He's pretty good."

"Good enough for varsity?" Coach Diego questioned.

"Yeah," Dylan responded. "Definitely."

"I think so too," Coach said. "Okay, thanks,

Fraiser. You can take off now. I want you to watch tryouts tomorrow too."

Dylan nodded. As the star goalie, he didn't need to try out. He had to admit that he liked being asked to watch the tryouts and give his opinion. Soccer was important to him, and Coach respected Dylan's dedication. *If only my dad cared half as much about what matters to me,* Dylan thought bitterly.

He jumped off the bleachers and headed down the field to where the water fountain was—and where the girls' team was holding try-outs. He was so curious about Laurel. He'd been hyperaware of her in poetry, the only class they had in common. He wondered if she was every-thing he imagined her to be. Just because she wore jeans and T-shirts and ate red meat and ap-preciated soccer didn't mean she ran deep, Dylan knew. Maybe she was as superficial as the rest. Into talking about sweet-sixteen parties and where she got her hair cut.

Dylan scanned the field, spotting Laurel right away. She was third in line, right after Ava. The first girl dribbled and kicked the ball at the goal, but goalie Amy easily blocked her shot. Ava kicked well, as always. Laurel's turn. She ran forward, ex-pertly dribbling the ball. And then she kicked— no, *whaled*—the ball forward. Amy dove for it, but she wasn't even close. It sailed straight into the goal.

Dylan's eyes widened. *Unbelievable*. He had never seen anyone, male or female, kick such a powerful, awesomely aimed shot before. Laurel ran to the back of the line, the rest of the girls observing her with awe. *Huh*. The girl got more interesting by the moment.

Did Cara warn her about me? Dylan wondered. *I hope not.*

Four

LAUREL JOGGED ACROSS the field to the girls' locker room, looking forward to getting home after her first day of school and the grueling soccer tryouts. But she couldn't resist slowing down as she passed the area where the guys' tryouts were. She was dying to get a glimpse of Dylan.

Tall, lanky, but muscular, with intense green eyes and thick, blond hair, Dylan Fraiser was one of the best-looking guys she'd ever seen. But more than that, there was something about him that got to her. Maybe it was the soccer thing. No. It was more than that. A sense of familiarity somehow.

She squinted as she looked around the field. She spotted a familiar face from her math class and from history, but she didn't see Dylan anywhere. *He probably didn't have to try out,* she realized.

"Hey, Laurel!"

Ava jogged to catch up with her. Surprised, Laurel stopped, pulling out her damp T-shirt so that it didn't cling to her sweaty body.

"You're incredible!" Ava exclaimed. "Where'd you learn to play like that?"

Laurel grinned at the compliment. "I don't know. I've been playing for a long time, I guess."

They began walking. "Well, you *definitely* made varsity," Ava said. "I hope I did too! Though thanks to you, *everyone* else looked awful!"

Laurel laughed. *Huh.* Another stereotype exploded. Not all gorgeous, popular girls were snobs. "You played great. You're especially great at defense."

Ava beamed. They headed inside the locker room. "Thanks. Oh, hey, a friend of mine from the guys' soccer team is having a party tomorrow night. Wanna come? You can talk soccer all night."

I bet Dylan will be there, Laurel thought.

"Sure!" she told Ava. "And thanks. Being the new girl, I really appreciate the invitation."

"No prob. I'll give you the address tomorrow. See ya!" And with that, Ava disappeared around a corner of lockers.

A party! She'd been invited to a party!

Laurel headed to her locker, slung her gym bag over her shoulder, and jogged back out. She couldn't wait to get home and tell her parents how much she liked her new school. How excited she was to be here. How much better the classes and facilities were than District's. Maybe she'd even tell her mom she already had a secret crush. She jogged the two miles home, full of energy despite the hard tryouts.

"Hey! I'm home!" she called out the moment she unlocked the door and rushed inside. She was greeted by dead silence. A note lay on the console table in the foyer.

Hi, sweetie, it read. *Hope you had a great first day and a good tryout! Mom's working late tonight, and I have a meeting. There's Chinese in the fridge if you're hungry. Love, Dad.*

Laurel crumpled up the piece of paper. So much for sharing her excitement with her parents. She knew they'd never be home when she got home from school, but she'd figured by now— six—*one* of them might be. Well, whatever. She could call Liza!

Laurel sprinted upstairs to her room, grabbed the cordless, jumped on her bed, and dialed. But after two rings Liza's answering machine clicked on. Disappointed, Laurel left a quick message and hung up.

Maybe Julie is around, Laurel thought, dialing her oldest sister's number.

"Hey, I'm not here right now, but—"

Another machine. Laurel clicked off, not bothering to leave a message. She sighed. She had to talk to *someone.* She picked up Harold, hugging the stuffed bear close to her body. She couldn't call Gavin. The sound of his voice would probably make her cry. Besides, he was probably on a hot date with Geena. And he might want details about her great new life.

Laurel's eyes fell on a black-and-white photo in a braided silver frame on her bureau. The three Bayer girls, Laurel, Julie, and Dani, as bridesmaids in their cousin Maggie's wedding a few years ago. All three wore the same hideous peach chiffon dress. Dani, of course, had loved the dress. Laurel and Dani disagreed on just about everything. Except about how necessary it was to talk about guys. Laurel dialed.

But once again an answering machine message blared in Laurel's ear. Didn't anyone stay home anymore? Dani would probably go on and on about sororities anyway. Her sister was consumed by rush week.

Laurel did have one more option, though. She put down the phone and booted up her computer. She could *write* to Liza and Julie and Dani and tell them all about her amazing day. And maybe there would be a response from Gavin. It might give her some satisfaction to know that he'd gotten her e-mail and thought she was having the time of her life. Which she was. Hadn't she had an incredibly successful first day?

There *was* a message from Gavin. Even just the sight of his e-mail address on her computer did strange things to her heart rate. With a click of the mouse, she opened it.

L:

I miss you. Last night on a date with Geena, I was telling her how strange it was that you're so far away. I have to admit, the girl knows how to comfort a guy! I wish I could come out for your birthday—I bet your party will be amazing. And good luck with the beach dude! Write back soon.

—G

Laurel blinked back the tears threatening to spill down her cheeks. *You didn't expect him to be jealous of an imaginary surfer, did you?*

Gavin probably wasn't even thinking about her. He was probably busy thinking about Geena. And Laurel had other things to think about too. Like how horrible she felt. About Gavin. About lying in her e-mail in the first place. About missing Liza.

Suddenly being invited to a party didn't seem like the answer to all her woes.

Five

DYLAN TRIED HARD to study the map of Asia on page fifty-four of his textbook, as he'd been doing for nearly an hour. But it was useless. The only geography that Dylan was interested in was Ohio.

Sitting on the floor with his back against his bed, Dylan put down the heavy book. He tried to imagine what Ohio was like, but he couldn't. Would Laurel be at the party tomorrow night? he wondered for the twentieth time. Ava and her crew had probably invited her. After all, Laurel was a sure shot for varsity soccer. Unless Ava and her friends were jealous of Laurel? Nah, Ava was okay. Dylan had a very strong feeling he'd see Laurel at the party. And he'd steal her away from the eagle eyes of her new friend, Cara.

Laurel didn't need protection from him. If

anything, Dylan would need protection from Laurel. It had been forever since he'd been so interested in a girl. And that meant his own feelings were at stake. An infrequent occurrence.

A knock at his door was followed by, "Dyl?"

Dad. Great. So much for daydreaming about Laurel Bayer. Dylan lugged the textbook back on his lap, flipped open to Asia, and pretended to be absorbed in the mountainous regions. "It's open."

His bedroom door swung open, and his dad popped in his blond head. "Ah, good to see you studying. I was going to ask how school was today, but I won't interrupt you. We'll talk over breakfast."

Dylan nodded, and his dad closed the door behind him.

Dylan mentally counted down from five. *Three . . . two . . . one.* The door opened again. "Hey, Dyl—you signed up for debate, right? It's crucial for your college applications."

Dylan nodded. "I did, Dad." He didn't lift his gaze. His father wouldn't want him to miss a single dot on the map, after all.

"Good. 'Night."

"'Night," Dylan whispered as the door closed behind his father. Typical. Totally typical. If he were with his mom, she'd have rushed to talk to him the minute he got home from school, asking about everything: his friends, his art teacher, if any girls had caught his eye.

He couldn't get Laurel's face off his mind. Her high cheekbones and heart-shaped face. Her huge, dark, expressive eyes. Her full lips. Her strong, toned legs kicking at the soccer ball.

Man. He shot up off the floor and pulled his sketch pad and a piece of charcoal out of his desk drawer, then sat at his swiveling chair. He lightly rubbed the charcoal against the white paper, creating intersecting soft lines. A half hour later he switched on his brass desk lamp and held the paper at arm's length, squinting at the beginnings of his drawing.

Hey, if he was going to think about Laurel's face all night, he might as well draw her.

Is the point *of this little flare skirt to make my legs look like tree trunks?* Laurel wondered as she stared in the full-length mirror attached to her closet door. She slipped off the skirt and tossed it onto her bed with ten other party-outfit rejects.

Back to good old jeans, she thought. *Could I be any more boring?* She put on her jeans and a new flower-trimmed tank top. *And could this day get any worse?*

Today had been the polar opposite of yesterday. She'd been completely overwhelmed at school. Cara had needed to see her adviser after homeroom, and Laurel couldn't seem to figure out how to get to first period by herself. She'd been late to class, calling extra attention to herself when everyone had already heard there was a new girl. Eyes had seemed to follow her wherever she went. A high point had been lunch, when Cara and Dave offered to drive her to tonight's party. She hadn't even thought about how she'd get there. The ride was a total lifesaver in more ways than one: She wouldn't have to go in alone.

She'd hoped Dylan would join them for lunch, but he hadn't, and he'd been late to poetry. Then he'd bolted right after class, so Laurel hadn't gotten a chance to talk to him again. She *had* been imagining his interest at lunch yesterday. No doubt Dylan would spend the entire evening talking to Ava. *If* he was even going.

Laurel brushed her hair, barely able to handle the movement. She was that sore. Soccer tryouts had been tough today, though she thought she'd done pretty well again.

Glancing at the clock, she realized Cara and Dave would be here any minute. Laurel slipped into her black suede clogs, applied some lip gloss, grabbed her all-purpose black cotton cardigan, then headed downstairs.

"Hi, honey." Ellie Bayer placed her black leather briefcase on the kitchen table. "Kiss for your mom?"

Laurel smiled and kissed her mom's soft cheek. She smelled of expensive perfume. "How was your day?"

"Nuts, but in a good way." Her mom ran a hand

through her short, chestnut-colored hair. "How about yours? How was day two?"

Lonely. Tiring. Overwhelming. Laurel shrugged. "Okay, I guess."

Her mom sat down at the table, slipped off her black heels, and began massaging her feet. "Hey, are you going somewhere? You look so nice."

Laurel stared at her mother. "*Hello?* I told Dad this morning that I was invited to a party. He said it was okay. Didn't he tell you?"

Mrs. Bayer wrinkled her face. "Oh—that's right! Gosh, I've got so much on my mind that I must have zonked on that one."

Zoned, Laurel corrected mentally.

"You'll be home by ten, right?" her mom asked. "It *is* a school night, Laurel."

You might congratulate me on the fact that I got invited to a party my first day of school, she thought, then felt instantly guilty. She knew her mom really did have a lot on her mind. "Ten on the dot, I promise." Laurel filled a glass with cold water and took a long, soothing drink. She decided to bring up the subject of her own party—now wouldn't be a worse time than any other. "So, um, speaking of parties . . ."

Her mom continued massaging her feet. She clearly hadn't gotten the hint.

"Mom? I mean my *birthday*. Are you and Dad planning anything?"

Mrs. Bayer glanced up with total surprise on her

face. "Um, of course, sweetie. Of course we're planning something."

Laurel blinked. Her mom's expression had given her away. She'd forgotten. Her mother had actually forgotten her sixteenth birthday! Wasn't that, like, illegal or something?

Mrs. Bayer jumped up and rushed over to Laurel, smoothing a strand of her hair behind her ear. "Honey, of course Daddy and I are going to do something special for your birthday. We just haven't had much time to figure out the details. Between the move and starting our new jobs and getting acclimated . . ."

Laurel heard a car pulling into the driveway, then a short honk. "That's my ride." She rushed toward the door. "I'll see you later."

"Laurel," her mom called after her.

She closed her eyes, then opened them and turned around. Her mom walked over to her and put both hands on her shoulders. "I love you, honey. Your dad and I would never let you down. You know that, right?"

Laurel nodded "I know." She threw her arms around her mom and squeezed.

After all, letting her down was Gavin's job.

There she was. Standing by herself at the far end of the deck, facing the Pacific. Under the moonlight and looking absolutely beautiful.

Dylan wished he had his sketch pad. He'd been at

Parker's party for twenty minutes, searching the vast beach house for Laurel. He'd seen her arrive with Cara and Dave, who he'd known were driving her, but then Laurel had been swallowed up in an endless round of introductions, and he'd lost track of her.

"Hi, Dylan!"

"Hi, Dylan!"

"Dylan, hi!"

He slipped away from the throng and headed across the deck to where Laurel stood. She stared out at the dark ocean, which was slightly illuminated by the terrace's lights.

"Got tired of saying 'nice to meet you,' huh?"

Laurel whirled around and flashed him a surprised grin. "Everyone at Hunt is so nice. But yeah. I've said 'nice to meet you' about a hundred times since getting here a half hour ago!"

"So how about a walk on the beach?" He gestured at the sand below.

Her entire face lit up. He smiled and led her down the steep wooden stairs to the sand. He stopped to untie his work boots. Laurel kicked off her clogs and ran across the beach toward the water.

Dylan dropped his boots and peeled off his socks. Spunky, wasn't she?

"This is so cool!" she called, rolling up the bottoms of her jeans and dipping her toes in the ocean. "Hey, it's actually warm!" She crouched down, splashing her hands in the water. "Why isn't everyone out here?"

Dylan made his way over to her. "Because this is nothing new." He dropped onto the sand a couple of feet from the shore, dug his bare feet into the cool sand, and rested his arms on his knees. "We go to the beach all the time. Southern California *is* the beach."

Laurel stood and put her hands on her hips as she gazed out at the breaking waves, her back to Dylan. "I can't imagine *this* ever getting old."

How Dylan wished he had that attitude. "Yeah, well, when you've been somewhere for too long, everything gets old."

Laurel glanced at Dylan, then walked toward him. "Have you lived here your whole life?"

"Yep." He scooped up some sand, then watched it fall through his fingers. "Except for when I was nine and ten and lived in Sydney."

"Australia?" Laurel asked, sitting down next to him.

He nodded. "My mom works for the UN. She'd just started her job then. My parents were still married, so my dad and I moved with her."

Laurel raised an eyebrow. "And now?"

Dylan stared at the ocean. "My dad got tired of following her to a different country every six months. Didn't think it was good for 'our son.' So they got divorced when I was twelve."

Laurel dug her feet into the sand. "Sorry."

"Yeah, me too," Dylan said. "Especially because I've been stuck living with my dad the last

46

four years. He gets me for school, and my mom gets me for the summer. I spent the past two months in Tel Aviv."

Laurel blinked. "Wow." She rested her chin on her knees. "That must be hard, though. Having your mom so far away."

"Sort of." Dylan picked up a shell, tracing its ragged edge with his finger. "Partly because the house with just me and my dad is kind of . . . intense." He tossed the shell into the water, then looked at Laurel. "But more because whenever I visit my mom, I don't want to come back."

The sound of a girl drunkenly shrieking with laughter suddenly pierced the air. Dylan glanced over his shoulder. Under one of the terrace's lights he could just make out Amanda tripping over her own feet and falling flat on her butt, then shrieking with laughter again.

"I'm so drunk!" she called out.

Dylan rolled his eyes. Did he already mention that it had been a colossal mistake to hook up with her? What had he been thinking?

Laurel lifted her hands out of the sand and rubbed them together. "We can go back, you know. I could sit out here all night, but I don't want to keep you from having fun."

Dylan shook his head, not taking his eyes off her. "I *am* having fun."

Laurel smiled. "Oh. Good. I mean, I am too." She moved her gaze to the ocean. For a long moment they were both quiet, the only sounds the crashing of the waves and the laughter and music drifting from the party.

Dylan stretched his legs out in front of him, psyched that Laurel wanted to hang out here with him and talk. About real stuff too. He'd been right to be attracted to her. He glanced at her; she was staring out at the water, fidgeting with the beaded bracelet around her wrist. A small part of him wanted to reach over and kiss her. Okay, a *big* part of him wanted to.

But that's how I usually start things with girls, Dylan realized. And he felt differently about Laurel, which probably meant he should handle things differently. *Like, maybe we should actually go out on a date.* That was, if Laurel wanted to, of course.

Plus the last thing he needed was for Cara to press Laurel about the details of their little beach fest and hear they'd made out. Cara would surely tell Laurel he was a player.

Laurel sighed, interrupting Dylan's rambling thoughts. "You know what? You've traveled all around the world, and this is the first time I've ever seen the Pacific Ocean. I've never even been to LA or any city, for that matter."

"Really?" Laurel had given him the perfect opener. He only hoped this wouldn't sound cheesy. As expert as he'd become at hooking up with girls, he'd never actually asked one out on a *date*.

Just do it already, he thought.

Whatever. Here goes. "Well . . . I could show you around. Maybe tomorrow night?"

"Yeah?" Laurel grinned. "That would be great!"

"Cool," Dylan said, trying to act as if it was no big deal. As if he *hadn't* been thinking about this girl for the past twenty-four hours and she hadn't just made his week. Possibly his month.

Dylan glanced up at the dark sky. And then he had to say it. He had to risk his coolness factor and express the thought that had popped into his mind. He cleared his throat. "You know, I think I'd like Grange, Ohio."

Laurel tilted her head. "Oh yeah? You're into having absolutely nothing to do?"

He laughed. He laughed so hard that she started cracking up too. He turned to her and smiled. "It's where you're from."

Laurel didn't say a word. But Dylan could tell from the way she was shyly smiling, her dimple out in full force, that he'd said the right thing. He and Laurel were off to a good start.

Now he just had to make it through the night without kissing her.

Six

"I'M HOME!" LAUREL called out as she walked through the front door at nine fifty-eight P.M. She couldn't wait to tell her parents about the party—the house, the beach, her date for tomorrow. . . .

But the house was dead quiet, and the only lights were in the hall and illuminating the stairs. She spotted a note on the hallway table in her mother's loopy handwriting.

It's nine forty-five. Dad and I waited up to hear about your party but then couldn't keep our eyes open another minute. Turn off the hall lights so we'll know you're home. Sweet dreams, Mom

Laurel crumpled up the piece of paper. So this was how her family was going to communicate now? Through notes and light signals? This was how they were going to plan her sweet-sixteen party?

Maybe Dylan will be your date, she thought. *Even if the party Mom and Dad throw is just family and maybe Cara, Dave, and even Ava. Wouldn't that be amazing?* A gorgeous, interesting date and friends! Laurel turned off the light and headed upstairs to her room, smiling all the way.

The cutest guy at Hunt asked me out, Laurel thought, flopping onto her bed. On the beach, no less. That sort of made what she'd e-mailed Gavin true! Laurel picked up Harold, hugging the worn-out stuffed bear to her chest. *And he likes me as more than as a friend!* she added mentally, squeezing Harold's brown fur as she tried to absorb that this was really happening

I'd like Grange, Ohio, because that's where you're from. . . .

Laurel sat up, realizing that things were actually starting to turn around. She reached for the phone and dialed Liza's number, vowing to stay on only a few minutes. Her parents would freak if they knew how often she was calling long-distance.

"Hello?" Liza answered.

"It's me," Laurel said. "Liza—I'm going out with the cutest guy in the world tomorrow night!"

"Oh, right!" Liza said. "The guy you e-mailed Gavin about. He told me you met some guy on the beach!"

Oops. Laurel's smiled faded. She hadn't realized Gavin would mention the e-mail to Liza. *That was dumb of you,* she thought. She suddenly envisioned

Gavin running into Liza in the hall at District, saying, *Hey, so Laur's having a blast in CA—she even met a guy already*. "Liza, Dylan did ask me out on the beach, but—I mean, I kind of exaggerated what I wrote to Gavin. I wanted him to think everything's okay, you know? That I'm not out here crying over him."

"Well, it sure sounds like you're not!" Liza said with a laugh. "So tell me all about Dylan!"

Laurel excitedly paced around her room as she told Liza every detail about the party and her conversation with Dylan. How when they talked, Dylan made intense eye contact. How he seemed quiet at times, but you could tell that his brain was churning at warp speed. How he'd traveled to all these amazing places. And of course, Laurel was sure not to leave out the sweet way he'd complimented her. And how extremely cute he was.

"Wow. That sounds incredible," Liza said. "*He* sounds incredible! So then what happened?"

Hello? Was Liza so tired that she'd completely missed what Laurel had just told her? She dropped down onto her desk char. "I told you—he asked me out."

"Yeah, but what about the kiss before you left?" Liza asked. "Was it amazing?"

Laurel's shoulders stiffened. She sat down on her bed, her back straight as a board. Dylan *hadn't* kissed her. He hadn't even attempted to. They'd hung out on the beach for a while longer, looking out at the ocean. They'd talked about soccer, and then Laurel realized that it was nine-forty and she'd better go. So Dylan had walked her up to the house, where Cara and Dave were waiting for her.

No kiss. All he'd said was, *See you tomorrow.* Then he smiled and disappeared into the crowd.

"Um, I think Dylan's the gentlemanly type," Laurel explained. "I have a feeling he wanted to wait till after our date." Laurel thought about that for a moment. Dylan Fraiser was polite and all, but Laurel wouldn't describe him to anyone as gentlemanly. He was more . . . the seductive type.

"Oh, I'm sure you're right," Liza said. "He does sound great."

Laurel stared blankly at her dark computer screen. *Or maybe he likes you as a friend, and you read the whole thing wrong,* she thought, her shoulders slumping.

Why *hadn't* Dylan tried to kiss her? They'd been alone on the beach for a very long time. Wouldn't most guys make a move? A kiss on the cheek, even? *Did I imagine everything tonight?* Laurel wondered, biting her lip. What if her conversation with Dylan hadn't really been romantic at all? What if it had just been . . . a conversation? Maybe he was just being nice when he'd said that thing about liking Ohio.

Laurel scrunched her eyes shut as she remembered the way that Dylan had "asked her out." *I could show you around,* he'd suggested. *Maybe tomorrow night?*

Oh God, Laurel thought, cringing. It was entirely possible that Dylan had just been asking her to hang out as friends. Maybe he wasn't the least bit attracted to her. Maybe she was sending off those dreaded platonic vibes again. Maybe, maybe, maybe!

"So you didn't tell me your parents were throwing you a major sweet sixteen!" Liza exclaimed. "Gavin told me all about it. It sounds awesome! Everyone from your class—cool Californians, Dylan . . . Oh, wait, I think I hear my mom. She'll freak if she knows I'm talking this late. . . ."

"Uh, Liza," Laurel said, beginning to sweat. "Um . . ." She had to tell Liza she'd made up all that so Gavin wouldn't think she was pining away for him. Liza would understand. But suddenly she couldn't bear to speak the truth. That there was no party. That her parents were too busy to even remember her birthday. That she couldn't bear to see Gavin and pretend everything was okay. That she'd misread everything that had happened with Dylan tonight.

You have to tell Liza the truth, Laurel thought. *She's your best friend. If you can't be a total lameoid with your best friend, then who can you be one with?*

"Liza, um, there's—"

"Uh-oh, gotta go," Liza interrupted in a panicked

voice. "My mom's coming. I'll call you tomorrow!"

Click. Laurel sighed and clicked off herself. She slumped over her desk; her head felt like it weighed a hundred pounds.

She'd tell Liza the truth tomorrow. For tonight, just tonight, she actually wanted to *believe* she was having that amazing sweet sixteen. With doting parents, new friends, and a cute, new adoring guy.

Just for tonight. Even if Dylan wouldn't be her date in a million years.

She's so pretty, Dylan thought, trying not to stare at Laurel. He sat across from her at a lunch table. Dave sat next to him, and Cara sat next to Laurel. Cara kept sending him weird looks. She knew.

Knew that he liked Laurel. Had Cara warned her about him? Laurel hadn't given him any strange looks, so perhaps he'd been worrying for nothing. He hadn't told Dave or Cara that he'd asked her out last night.

As Laurel munched on pretzels and listened to Dave's funny story about biology class, Dylan took the opportunity to further appreciate her purple V-necked top, which showed off an enticing expanse of her skin. He also noticed she was wearing little sun-shaped silver earrings.

Laurel glanced down at her watch, which looked enormous on her narrow wrist. "Ooh. I gotta go!" She stood up and grabbed her knapsack. "I told Ms. Lopez I'd meet with her before next period."

"To talk about 'creating future goals,'" Cara said knowingly, imitating the teacher's solemn way of speaking.

Laurel laughed as she reached for her lunch tray. "Exactly."

Dylan touched Laurel's arm. "You can leave that here. I'll bus it for you."

Such a heavy silence overtook the table that you would have thought Dylan had just offered to give Laurel a pedicure. A blush started to creep up his neck as he felt Cara and Dave's eyes bore into him.

What's the problem? Dylan wondered, shifting in his seat. Couldn't he do something nice for the girl?

Laurel smiled. "Thanks! See you guys later."

"Later," Dylan returned.

Dylan watched her walk off. When he returned his attention to his friends, he noticed that his table was again overcome by silence. "What?" he demanded, a bit embarrassed.

Dave's dark brown eyes twinkled. "*'I'll bus it for you'?*" he repeated, incredulous.

Cara crossed her arms over her chest. "I like her, Dylan," she stated, staring him down.

Dylan shook his head. "Yeah, well, so do I. So what's the problem?"

Cara wagged a finger at him, her silver bracelets jangling against each other. "I will *not* let you play Laurel the way you play every other girl."

"Whoa. Whoa. Calm down," Dylan said. So he

had been worried for a reason. Cara could be downright dangerous when she got like this. "First of all, this isn't a matter of you 'letting me.' But second, I don't intend to play Laurel at all. I really like her."

Cara rolled her eyes. "Great. You don't *intend* to."

Dave smirked, balancing his chair on its two back legs. "Right. And I don't *intend* to go to class next period."

Dylan sighed, frustrated. Did his friends really think he was this much of a jerk? Okay, fine, he didn't have the most stellar track record when it came to girls. But didn't at least *Dave* know that when Dylan found a girl he could really like, really talk to, he'd be *hers*? "Look, it's different this time. I'm *not* going to play her," he insisted. More eye rolls and smirks. What would it take for them to believe him? "I asked her out, okay? On a date. For tonight."

Both his friends' expressions quickly lost their attitude. Dave dropped his chair down on all four legs.

"You asked her out?" Cara's eyes widened, her face softening. "On a real date?"

Dylan nodded. Maybe he *was* worse than he thought.

"So you really like her," Cara said. Not a question, a statement.

Finally. Dylan pushed his tray in front of him and leaned back, stretching his legs out in front of

58

him. "Yes. That's what I've been saying."

Cara grinned. "Okay, Dylan. I believe you."

"Gee, thanks." Dylan shook his head. "I didn't know I was such an evil jerk who you couldn't trust around a friend of yours."

Cara tilted her head. "Hardly an evil jerk. But hardly someone I'd trust with the heart of a friend. And that's your own fault, Dylan Fraiser, so don't act all hurt about it on me now."

Dave shrugged.

"But I think you're serious," Cara said. "I know you've never asked a girl out on a real date before. To you, hooking up means making out wherever you happen to be. So if you asked Laurel out, it's a sign you're truly interested in her as a person."

Finally again, Dylan thought.

"Ooh! This is so great." Cara inched her chair closer to Dylan's. "Okay. So you know what you have to do, right? You know you have to take it slow."

"I know," Dylan agreed. "I *am* taking it slow. I mean, I didn't even make a move last night on the beach."

Cara arched an eyebrow. "And . . . ?"

Dylan stared at her, confused. "And what?"

"And what about tonight?" she asked. "You're going to take it slow again, right?" She stared at Dylan.

But he didn't exactly get what she meant. "Well,

I'm taking her out. And I mean, I'm really attracted to her, so—"

"So, the guy is *not* going to take it slow," Dave interrupted, flashing a grin and reaching out to slap Dylan five. "It's not his style. And then tomorrow morning he'll be, like, Laurel *who?*"

Dylan looked from Cara to Dave and back again. Wow. So even Dave truly believed he couldn't commit to a girl. *Have I really been that bad?* he wondered for the tenth time. *Maybe so. I thought I was justified, but now I'm just coming across as a real schmuck. The kind of guy who uses girls, then acts all distant the next morning.* He suddenly wondered how many girls he'd hurt. Had he hurt Amanda, for instance? She acted so nonchalant about the whole thing, but maybe that was just attitude. Maybe she had been putting on an act because she didn't want him to know he'd hurt her.

"Well, going slow is your new style, then," Cara said. "If you like Laurel, Dylan, then show her—by not making a move tonight."

What the heck was she talking about? "I don't get it. If I really like Laurel, shouldn't I just go for it?" That seemed fairly logical, didn't it?

"That's what you usually do," Cara argued. "If you like Laurel and want to go out with her, you need to build a relationship based on trust, not making out or whatever." Cara pulled a pack of Trident out of her bag and offered a piece to Dylan and Dave, who both stuck out their hands. "That's what Dave and I did."

"Aw, babe," Dave said, popping the gum in his mouth. "You don't need to go telling him *that*."

Dylan grinned, enjoying seeing his friend's macho cover get blown. Then he looked back at Cara, wanting to return to the topic at hand. Namely, him and Laurel. "So you're saying that I absolutely *shouldn't* make a move tonight?"

"I'm saying that for once, you might want to actually get to know a girl before you jump her bones," Cara stated. Dylan flinched at her bluntness, but Cara simply shrugged. "Besides, you never know. Laurel might've heard about your reputation. In which case, you're going to have to prove that you really like her and you're *not* just after her body."

"So you didn't tell her?" Dylan asked.

"Hey, you're my bud," she said. "You're my boyfriend's best friend. I'd never trip you up, Dylan—not before you're even out of the gate." Cara stood up and patted Dylan on the back. "Your past might've caught up with you, though, my friend."

"Ouch," Dave commented. "She does have a point."

Yeah, Dylan thought, swallowing. *She does.* He'd worried about Cara telling Laurel to be on guard with Dylan. He hadn't even thought about the fact that a lot of girls at Hunt could tell Laurel the same thing.

And then she might go straight to Cara, asking if it were true.

And Cara would have to say yes. She might vouch for him, but she'd still have to say it was all true.

Nice way to learn a lesson, Dylan thought. *Just when you were ready to change.*

Seven

To SAY THAT Laurel was happy that soccer try-outs were over for the day would have been a supreme understatement. Actually, tryouts were over, period. There were only so many slots, but so many girls had tried out that the coach had to keep whittling out the girls by having them compete against each other. On Monday, Coach Martin would be posting the lucky bunch who'd made it.

But that wasn't why Laurel was unbelievably excited as she started to walk off the field with some of her maybe teammates, butterflies fluttering around in her stomach. No, Laurel was psyched because now that soccer was over, she was even closer to having her date with Dylan.

And she actually felt comfortable calling it that: a date. Her mind drifted off into her own thoughts as the other girls chattered around her. Thankfully, the anxiety attack that Laurel had last night had been completely reversed by Dylan's actions toward her today.

He was so attentive, Laurel thought, remembering how Dylan had offered to bus her tray at lunch. And then he'd passed her a note in poetry class, asking if seven-thirty would be a good time for him to pick her up. If this wasn't a date, Laurel didn't know what was. *And it's only a couple of hours from now,* she realized, looking up at the cloudless blue sky. She hugged herself, excitement washing over her.

"You're awfully quiet, Laurel," Ava observed as she strolled up next to her.

Laurel shrugged breezily, still lost in her happy haze. "Just thinking."

Ava smiled. "Looks like you're having some pretty happy thoughts there."

Laurel toyed with her purple beaded bracelet. "Yeah. I guess I am."

As they neared the guys' practice area, Laurel noticed that the guys' team was still playing on the field. She couldn't help scanning the area for Dylan. She found him easily enough. He was right where he was supposed to be—in front of the goal. Dylan was looking pretty cute with his thick, blond hair all ruffled and messy, his loose black nylon shorts hanging over a pair of biking shorts, and his gray T-shirt hugging his body ever so slightly. *A very nice-looking body,* Laurel thought.

At the moment one of the guys on the team took aim at the goal, kicking it full speed ahead. As fast as lightning, Dylan dove for the ball, blocking the goal, rolling over on his back as he did so.

Not a bad goalie either, Laurel decided as she watched him appreciatively.

Ava and a couple of the other girls cheered as they passed by. "Way to go, Fraiser!" Ava hollered.

Jumping up, Dylan glanced over his shoulder, jutting out his chin in thanks. Then, noticing Laurel, he smiled. Those flutters in her abdomen intensifying, Laurel grinned back. Tonight was going to be so much fun!

"Dylan gets hotter every year," commented Jenny Meyer, who was walking behind Laurel and Ava as Dylan turned back around to block another shot.

"Mmm. Sure has," Ava added, watching him as they continued to walk.

Laurel bit back a smile, feeling her cheeks flame up. Part of her wanted to tell them everything, but the better part of her resisted. Nothing more deadly to a fledgling romance than telling everyone about it. It was almost as if talking about her date might jinx it. And Laurel was not about to let that happen.

Still, she couldn't stop herself from trying to find out the scoop on Dylan. "So why don't any of you guys go out with him?" she asked, trying to sound nonchalant.

Ava laughed, wiping some sweat off her forehead. "Oh, we all have." Her green eyes twinkled with amusement.

"Yeah. If you can call it that," Amy put in.

Suddenly Laurel's stomach tumbled down to the grass. They'd *all* gone out with him? That's not exactly what Laurel had wanted to hear. "What? What do you mean?"

Jenny jogged up so that she was walking in between Laurel and Ava. "Dylan's a total player," she explained, tossing her blond, curly hair behind her shoulder. "Relationships are *not* his thing."

"But hooking up is," Ava put in as they neared the locker-room doors. "And I must say, he's quite good at it."

Ava and Jenny both laughed as they all walked inside. Meanwhile Laurel felt positively nauseous.

Dylan was a *player?*

He *used* girls?

I pegged him all wrong, Laurel thought, slowly making her way over to the cream-colored locker where she'd stowed her bag.

"I'd live to see the day Dylan really falls for a girl. You know, takes her out on a date and everything," Jenny commented, swinging open the locker across from Laurel's. "Can you imagine *Dylan* on an actual date?"

Laurel glanced at Jenny, her heart sinking. *Wonderful.* Laurel dropped down onto the narrow wooden bench, staring at the rusty number 18 on her locker. Listlessly she untied her sneakers. So this *wasn't* a date tonight. Apparently Dylan never went on dates. *Perfect. I'm stuck in the friend role,* Laurel thought, tossing her shoes on the gray linoleum floor.

Because he sure hadn't tried to hook up with her last night, she reminded herself.

What is it with me? she wondered. *Why is it that every time I like a guy, he doesn't feel that way about me? Why am I so different from all these girls?*

It wasn't that she wanted to be one of Dylan's "girls," but she wouldn't mind being wanted a little bit.

Ava, whose locker was right next to Laurel's, turned to face her, tapping a pale pink nail against her chin. "You know, come to think of it, you just might be Dylan's next victim."

Laurel rolled her eyes. *Yeah, right.* That's why Dylan, the renowned hookup king, hadn't so much as caressed her pinkie the other night. "Doubtful," she muttered, pulling off her sweat-soaked ankle socks.

"Hey, I know these things," Ava insisted, sitting down next to Laurel. She reached into her knapsack and pulled out a little tub of lip balm, then applied some to her lips. "I can see them a mile away." Ava smacked her lips together. "Dylan's been checking you out. No question."

Laurel's dark eyes widened. Ava held out the tub of balm, offering some to Laurel. Laurel shook her head as her heart began to swell. Even though her better instincts warned against it, even though her past experiences warned against it, Laurel couldn't stop herself.

She smiled. And once again she had hope.

Until she realized she wouldn't win either way. If Dylan tried to kiss her tonight, it meant he'd totally ignore her tomorrow; he'd already have moved on to another "victim." And if he didn't try to kiss her, then her worst fears would be confirmed.

She wasn't the kind of girl guys were interested in.

So Dylan—who'd managed to push Gavin out of her mind for an entire day—would end up being a "friend" or someone who ducked her in the halls.

Great.

A few hours later Laurel was viewing the Dylan situation from an entirely new perspective. One that made her feel a lot better about everything. *Sort of.*

She stood in her closet, twirling a strand of hair around her finger so tightly that it almost cut off her circulation, trying to figure out what to wear tonight. She reached for her slim-fitting black satin pants, the ones she'd worn to Dani's graduation party in June.

After having some time to absorb Ava and Jenny's comments, Laurel had been able to sort out the facts. Which were:

1. Dylan was a player.
2. He didn't usually go out with girls on dates.

3. He'd asked her out on what was clearly a date.
4. He'd either make a move or not.

But what had made her feel better was the realization that:

5. If he didn't make a move, it meant he *liked* her. Just plain old liked her. And what was so terrible about that? It wasn't as if she'd known him her whole life and then suddenly developed feelings for him and he'd turned her down.

He was just a guy she'd met during her first week at school, who'd been nice enough to offer to show her some sights.

Nothing wrong with that.

Laurel unfolded her pants. And maybe, just maybe, Dylan liked her enough to ask her out on a date. Maybe, for the first time, he was interested in a relationship instead of simply a hookup.

Maybe. It was this particular *maybe* that Laurel had all of her hopes pinned on as she wriggled into her pants.

The phone rang. As usual, Laurel was the only one home. After sucking in her stomach so that she could snap her pants closed, Laurel walked over to her desk and picked up the black cordless phone. "Hello?"

"Hi, *chica!* Ready for your date?" Liza asked.

That was the question of the day, wasn't it?

Laurel's response had changed so many times over the past couple of hours, she almost didn't know how to feel. "I guess," she said, kicking at a stray black sock on the floor.

"You *guess?* What's wrong? You sound bummed."

Laurel searched her dresser for the burgundy top that looked good with these pants. "I'm not bummed. I'm just . . . totally confused." She crouched down, fishing through the drawers. And without waiting for Liza's prompt, Laurel dove into the Dylan saga and explained all of her conflicting emotions and concerns.

When Laurel had finally finished, Liza immediately said, "I'm with you. I like the sounds of that last *maybe.*"

Laurel laughed. "Hang on a minute—I have to put on my shirt." Laurel placed the cordless on her bed, quickly slipped on the shirt, then picked up the phone. "So you don't think I'm a fool for thinking there's a possibility?"

"Definitely not. He's given you so many signs."

Laurel stood in front of the mirror to check out her ensemble, but she couldn't focus on her reflection. "I guess . . . I just—"

"What? Oh, wait a minute. I know what you're so worried about. Your sweet sixteen! Dylan's your fantasy date for your big shindig!"

Laurel froze. She'd completely forgotten about her intention to set Liza straight about the lie she'd told Gavin.

"Liz—"

"Confidence, girl!" Liza interrupted. "I mean, are you forgetting how great you are? Perfect example is what you've accomplished already. You're having an amazing sweet sixteen with a ton of new friends, and you've only been in California for a couple of weeks!"

Laurel slumped down on her bed. *If only it were true,* she thought, unable to speak. Her throat tightened as tears threatened. "Um—"

"I just thought of something else," Liza exclaimed. "All that stuff about him being a player?"

Laurel gnawed her lower lip. "Yeah?"

"Ignore it. It might be true, but just because the guy has a past that doesn't mean he's not interested in having a relationship with somebody. The *right* somebody. And maybe that's you. How's *that* for a *maybe?*"

Laurel smiled weakly. "Thanks, Liza. I'll call tomorrow and tell you how it went." *And that I lied,* Laurel added mentally. *That there is no sweet sixteen. No ton of friends.*

And, she was sure, no fantasy date named Dylan dancing with her.

"Good luck!" Liza said, and clicked off.

Laurel stared into the mirror, her reflection sharply coming into focus. At least she looked okay. This outfit always made her feel good. All she had to do was find her strappy black sandals and she'd be set.

71

She wondered about what Liza had said. *Could* she possibly be that somebody? That girl who would change Dylan from player to potential boyfriend?

Or was that as much a fantasy as him being her birthday date?

"So, how does Mexican sound?" Dylan asked as he turned onto the freeway.

"I love Mexican!" Laurel said, grinning.

"Great." He speeded up into the rush of traffic. "I know a really great restaurant in Santa Monica. The food's good, but even better, the place has killer views."

"Sounds really amazing," she said.

Dylan turned to glance at her; she flashed him a smile. She looked so beautiful and happy that he nearly drove right into a palm tree, his car swerving toward the curb. "Oh. Sorry about that." He quickly recovered the wheel and turned into the parking lot of the hotel that the restaurant was in.

Man. This was so totally weird. Ever since he'd picked her up and seen how gorgeous and totally sexy she looked, he had actually been nervous. And even though they'd been driving for about twenty minutes, Dylan's nervousness hadn't worn off in the slightest. That never happened.

Well, okay, Dylan had been nervous around a girl twice before. But once was when he'd gone to the prom as a freshman . . . with a senior. Nervousness was understandable then. Accepted, even. And the other time was when his mother's friend's daughter—who was a twenty-something model—had given Dylan a tour of Paris. She'd been interesting, but they'd had nothing in common, nothing to say to each other, and they could barely communicate.

But Laurel was his age. And they had a lot to say to each other.

Dylan pulled into the parking lot, reaching out to take the ticket from the machine in the entrance. The red automatic gate rose, and he drove up the ramp to look for a space. Maybe this was what dating was all about. Maybe you were supposed to be nervous. If that was the case, Dylan wasn't sure he was game.

So this was what it felt like to really, really like someone, he thought. The nervousness, the sweaty palms, the inability to stop thinking about the person even when she was sitting right next to you.

He wondered if she could tell.

Dylan took a deep breath, and the weird churning in his stomach subsided. "We're here."

"Wow!" Laurel said as she got out of the car and stared up at the hotel.

"The restaurant's in the tower," he explained.

Laurel didn't take her eyes off the glass elevator that rose from the ground to the fiftieth floor. "Are we going to ride in that?"

Dylan smiled and nodded.

Laurel's face burst into a huge smile. "Wow!" she exclaimed again. Her excitement touched him. More than touched him. It had been a long time since he'd been psyched about something new, something fun.

They stepped into the elevator, which was like having a giant window onto the city of Santa Monica. From the awestruck expression on Laurel's face as she looked around, Dylan knew that he had chosen the right place to take her to.

"This is so cool," she said, pressing her fingertips to the glass and staring out as the elevator lifted them higher and higher and the view become more and more impressive. From the three different angles of the elevator, you could see the Santa Monica beach and boardwalk endlessly stretching out, the pier and its lighted rides and Ferris wheel. It was breathtaking. Plus you could see the lights of the city—buildings and houses glowing in the dark and getting smaller the higher the elevator rose. It almost seemed magical. Kind of like a ride in Disneyland.

"My parents used to take me here a lot when I was little," Dylan said. "I've always liked it."

"I can see why." Laurel beamed at him, then continued to stare out at the view, playing with a strand of her dark hair.

Dylan watched her silently, wanting more than anything to just grab her and kiss her. To put his hand on that gentle curve of her long neck. He was standing so close that he could smell the fruitiness of her shampoo. But as hard as it was, Dylan held back, stuffing his hands in his pockets.

There was no question in Dylan's mind that he was going to kiss Laurel tonight. He didn't have *that* much restraint. But he'd at least wait until *after* their date to make his move.

Still, he couldn't resist letting Laurel know how he felt. "You know, you look really great tonight."

Laurel tilted her head to look at Dylan. She smiled.

As Dylan gazed at her, he felt like everything was happening in slow motion. Like he could just reach over and kiss her . . .

"Thanks . . . so do you," she said, her eyes shyly darting down to the floor.

It was a good thing that the elevator door opened at that moment because Dylan was becoming dangerously close to reneging on his promise of no predinner kisses.

Dylan and Laurel were met by the delicious aromas of Mexican food and the fun roar of loud music and people talking and laughing. Topper's was a popular place, especially on weekends. It was more fun than elegant, which was why Dylan liked it so much.

The host led Dylan and Laurel to a corner table next to the floor-to-ceiling windows, which, like the elevator, showed off an incredible view of Santa Monica and the beach. As the host handed them their menus, Dylan silently sent the guy a man-to-man thanks. He couldn't have picked a more prime table.

"Enjoy your dinner, folks," the host said, walking off.

Laurel beamed at Dylan across the blue-and-white checkerboard-tiled table. "This place is great." She sat back in her chair, her impossibly big eyes glancing around the room. "Dylan, you couldn't have chosen a more fun place. I get great Mexican food and incredible views at the same time!"

Dylan smiled. That was exactly how he felt about Topper's. Another girl might have complained that it wasn't elegant enough or that their waiter hadn't appeared yet. But Laurel, as expected, simply seemed happy to be here.

She hugged her menu to her chest, her dark eyes twinkling. "I'm starving!"

"Me too," he said. "So, did you go to restaurants like this back in Ohio?"

Laurel laughed, picking up her napkin and placing it on her lap. "There *aren't* restaurants like this in Ohio. Not in Grange, at least."

"Hmmm. Just good old Wendy's, huh?" Dylan teased, rolling up the sleeves of his blue button-down shirt.

Laurel nodded, pointing at Dylan with her

menu. "If you're lucky, maybe I'll take you there sometime."

Dylan thought that going to Wendy's in Ohio *would* be a good time as long as Laurel was involved. A busboy delivered a bowl of blue corn chips and another one filled with salsa.

"Yum," Laurel said, snagging a chip full of salsa.

As Dylan leaned forward and dipped a chip too, a supercheesy soft-rock song came over the restaurant's Muzak system. He shook his head. "I've *never* been a fan of Topper's music selection," he complained, popping the chip into his mouth.

Laurel grinned. "This is pretty bad! I guess we'll just have to talk so much that we stop hearing it."

Dylan laughed and opened his menu. "Good idea." Laurel was so cool. So refreshing. So . . . exactly what he'd been looking for. He glanced down at the menu, afraid that she could tell he was thinking nonstop about her. "So, it seems like you're doing really well at Hunt."

"I haven't had any exams yet."

"No," he said, chuckling. "I mean socially. I've noticed you walking in the halls with a lot of different girls, like Cara, of course, and Jenny and Ava. They're all really cool."

Laurel frowned. But then her expression changed back to normal so quickly, he wasn't sure she'd frowned at all. Had he said something wrong?

Laurel glanced down at her menu. He had said something wrong. But what?

"I mean, they're all popular," Dylan added. "Ava's one of the most popular girls at Hunt."

She glanced up at him and tilted her head. What was she thinking? Did Ava say something about him?

"They're really nice," Laurel said as she glanced back down at the menu. She twisted a strand of hair around her finger. "I can see becoming friends with them."

Ava had said something. Or one of the other girls had. Or maybe he was just being paranoid.

Laurel seemed to be deciding what to order, so Dylan glanced down at his own menu and tried to make a decision.

Maybe the shrimp fajitas? Or the burrito combo was always good . . .

"Speaking of Ava," Laurel began. "She and I talked about you today."

Oh no. Dylan looked at Laurel. *Not good.*

Laurel's tone was a bit stiff. Forced. What the heck had Ava told her? That he'd hooked up with her and practically every girl at Hunt? That he wasn't interested in relationships? That getting your hopes up about Dylan Fraiser would bring you nothing but heartache?

"Talked about me?" he asked, dipping another chip as though he had no idea what she might say. As though he expected her to say something related to soccer. "About what?"

"She, um, mentioned that you guys sort of . . . went out." A tinge of color spread across Laurel's cheeks. She moved her gaze to her glass of water, staring at it as if it held the answers to life.

It's your own fault, he thought once again. *You are a hookup artist.*

His stomach twisted into knots. It was true that he and Ava had made out a bunch of times at the beginning of last year. But Dylan wouldn't call *that* going out. And the idea that he and Ava had hooked up in the past seemed to be making Laurel very uncomfortable. "We didn't really *go out,*" Dylan clarified.

Laurel's blush deepened. "She said that too. That you wouldn't really call it *'going out.'*"

Dylan gripped his menu. *Man.* Why would Ava tell Laurel *that?* Did she make a habit of exposing all of her past hookups to every new person she met?

So Cara had been right. Dylan's reputation *had* preceded him. Laurel obviously thought that he was a hookup artist. And now he was going to have to prove himself to her.

Dylan eyed her as she continued to read her menu. He wanted to say something, but anything he thought of just sounded stupid. Finally he managed, "Yeah, well, that was a long time ago. I'm not seeing anyone now."

Laurel glanced up, biting her lip. "Oh, um, I'm sorry. I shouldn't have brought it up. It's not like it matters."

But Dylan could tell by the strained tone of Laurel's voice that it *did* matter. And that she knew he was a player. Suddenly he was surprised she hadn't canceled the date.

Now what was he going to do?

"Hello, señor, señorita! Are you ready to order?"

Dylan glanced up at the waiter, who wore a goofy sombrero. Suddenly the lighthearted mood of the restaurant didn't fit the mood at the table. He was grateful for the interruption, though. "Ready, Laurel?"

She nodded, closing her menu and handing it to the waiter. "I'll have a California burrito with rice and beans on the side and a virgin margarita."

"I'll have a virgin margarita too," Dylan told him, "and the steak fajitas."

"Excellent choices," the waiter said. "I'll be right back with your drinks."

Laurel smiled—sort of a frozen smile.

Dylan sighed, leaning back in his seat.

Well, one thing had just become painfully clear to him.

There was no way he could kiss Laurel tonight.

Eight

IDIOT! LAUREL MENTALLY yelled at herself.

She glanced nervously at Dylan. His gaze was firmly focused on the road ahead as they exited the freeway for Pasadena. And he was silent, his mouth a straight line, as it had been for the past five minutes, ever since they left Topper's.

Why did she bring up what Ava had told her? That was so dumb!

You brought it up because you wanted him to put your mind at ease, to tell you none of that stuff was true. Or that it was a misunderstanding. That he was misunderstood.

But he hadn't said any of that. He'd simply become stiff and quiet, and they'd never recovered.

Laurel stared out her window and focused on the passing dark scenery. She toyed with the lock on her door, trying to make sense out of the evening. If only she'd kept her mouth shut.

Their date had started off so wonderfully! From the moment he'd picked her up at her house, she'd felt a sense of magic. She'd wished her parents had been home to meet him; they would have been really impressed. She'd been unable to take her eyes off him. He'd dressed up for the date in a pair of khakis and a crisp, button-down shirt. It had struck her that his attire possibly indicated that he considered this a date. Possibly. Anyway, it had definitely started things off on a good note.

And then the two of them had clicked, easily falling into conversation. He'd taken her to that amazing restaurant. She'd felt so comfortable with him. So . . . happy. She'd forgotten all about being the new girl, about Gavin, about the lie she hadn't corrected to Liza . . . about the birthday that would go uncelebrated.

All she could think about was Dylan and the way he made her feel. Pretty . . . listened to, and maybe even *wanted*. As a girl. Not as a friend.

Dylan turned right onto Palm Grove. Laurel recognized the street. They weren't far from her house. And soon their date would be over. *If that's what this even is,* she thought, her stomach sinking.

"That's the road to the Huntington Library," Dylan said, pointing to a turnoff to the left. "It's famous. The grounds are amazing."

Laurel was happy and relieved that he'd broken the silence. The name sounded vaguely familiar to her. "It's a museum?" she asked, ducking her head so that she could see the street Dylan referred to.

"And a library. It was originally a railroad magnate's estate. It has these really cool gardens." Dylan ran a hand through his hair, taking his eyes off the road for a moment to glance at Laurel. "We should go sometime so you can check it out."

Laurel blinked. "That would be great."

Hope bloomed. Maybe he didn't hate her after all. Maybe she'd simply upset him by bringing up his past record?

Maybe, maybe, maybe again!

But still . . . was this new invitation meant as a date or not? What was he thinking?

Laurel had a million questions, a ton of insecurities, no answers—and no clue how to just ask him what was up.

Stop being such a whiny baby! she ordered mentally. She settled back against the beige upholstered seat. *The guy likes you.*

(Or did, before you opened your big mouth.)

He asked you out for tonight, right? And what guy wasted a Friday night showing a school friend around Santa Monica? Taking her to the top-floor restaurant of a hotel with amazing views? And what guy would hint about future dates?

Unless that wasn't a date either . . .

Get a grip, Laurel, she told herself. *The guy gave you an opening. Take it. Say something.*

"I like your ring," she told him, reaching over to touch the thick piece of silver.

Dylan's hand jumped.

Laurel immediately drew back her own hand, her cheeks flushing. *And then again, maybe not,* she thought, her eyes darting toward the window. If this was how he reacted when she simply touched his arm . . .

"I, uh, bought it in Jerusalem this past summer," Dylan said, glancing at her. "In the old city."

Suddenly Laurel wished she could disappear through a secret door in her seat. *He* doesn't *like me,* she realized, noticing the way Dylan was now gripping onto the steering wheel so tightly that his knuckles were white. Obviously the physical contact—the *unbelievably slight* physical contact—had made him uncomfortable.

Which, considering the fact that he was supposedly a total player, could mean only one thing.

He was definitely *not* into her. *At least you know for sure now,* she thought.

Dylan pulled his car to a stop in front of Laurel's house. As he shifted into park, he turned to look at her. "Well . . . I had a great time tonight."

Laurel froze for a second. That was unexpected. Plus there was that intense, unwavering gaze again. That look that seemed to say, *I am totally into you.* Maybe that was simply Dylan's "look."

Or maybe she'd read the entire night wrong— the bad part anyway.

You're maybe-ing again, she told herself.

"Me too." Laurel smiled slightly, gazing back at him. Ever so slowly, she leaned in slightly closer to him. And he did the same, moving forward, inching closer to Laurel's face, to her mouth, so close that she could smell a hint of his spicy aftershave. . . . *He's going to kiss me,* Laurel thought, her heart thumping against her rib cage. *He's going to—*

Turn on the radio?

He pushed buttons on the dial until he found a station he liked. The car filled with Smashmouth. Then he settled back into his seat, his hands both on the steering wheel.

Laurel blinked, speechless, her heart rapidly plummeting to her stomach. What a fool she was! She'd thought he was going to kiss her, and all he wanted was a good song! Talk about embarrassing.

So was that it? Was she simply supposed to get out of the car now?

"Anyway, it was fun hanging out," Dylan said, gazing straight ahead through the windshield.

He was basically telling her to get out of his car. Could he seem any more bored and done with her?

Suddenly he turned to face her. "I'm really glad you moved to Pasadena."

Laurel, whose brain was still spinning from everything that had occurred in the past few minutes, allowed herself one last surge of hope.

She locked eyes with him. He looked so serious,

as though he had something more, something . . . important to say. Maybe now would be the moment she was waiting for.

"I really mean that," he added with a smile. "I could use another good friend."

Laurel swallowed, gripping onto the seat cushion. The *f* word. Her heart twisted and turned, but she managed to force a smile. "Yeah." Her palms sweating, she reached for the door handle. "Me too."

"Let me walk you to the door," Dylan offered, removing his seat belt.

Not able to share the same space with him a moment longer without breaking down, Laurel squeaked out, "No, that's okay, really." She pulled the metal handle, but the car door didn't budge. She tried again. No luck. *Oh. Right. The lock.* Embarrassment morphed into total humiliation. She quickly popped open the lock, then swung open the door. "Well, good night," she said, stepping out of the car.

Dylan smiled, switching the car into first. "Good night. Sweet dreams."

Sweet dreams? Yeah, right, Laurel thought, heading for the steps to her house. Her stomach dropped as she heard Dylan drive off, and she fumbled with her keys. It seemed to take her forever to fit the stupid key in the door.

Her heart twisting and turning, Laurel finally managed to unlock the door and walk inside. The house was dark and quiet; her parents had gone to a movie and weren't due home for another hour. For once, though, she didn't mind being alone. She was too depressed to talk to anyone else anyway.

At least I found out, she thought, trudging up the carpeted stairs. *At least I know for sure.* After all, Dylan had obviously wanted to make it clear that he only liked her as a friend. *That's probably why he got all awkward and weird,* she realized, pushing open the door to her room. He wasn't angry that she'd brought up what Ava said. He was simply worried that Laurel liked him, and he didn't know how to react.

Sighing shakily, Laurel collapsed belly down on her four-poster bed. This night was a disaster. But one thing was for sure. She was not going to let the Gavin situation happen to her all over again.

Not only wouldn't she reveal her crush, she wasn't going to let herself fall for him at all. *No way.* She'd be friends with Dylan—and expect nothing more. No matter how many times he gave her that heart-melting look with those intense green eyes of his, no matter how many great conversations they had, Laurel was not going to let herself get hurt.

Laurel rolled onto her back and picked up her loyal teddy bear. She stared at Harold's shiny black eyes, then hugged the bear to her chest.

Why was it that despite all that was new in her life, nothing was changing for her at all?

★　　　★　　　★

Dylan was consumed by one thought as he lay in bed that night. Well, actually there were many thoughts circling his brain, but they all had to do with one, single, overreaching topic: kissing Laurel.

Or rather, what it would be like to kiss Laurel since Dylan didn't actually know.

He kicked off his gray cotton comforter as he thought about how many times he'd wanted to grab Laurel and kiss her tonight. Almost everything she did, everything she said, whether the girl was smiling or completely serious, turned him on.

And not once had she lapsed into superficial conversation the way other girls did—talking about people in a catty way or going into a rapture over some trendy new clothing label. There was always so much light and laughter in Laurel's face . . . in her eyes. Dylan had a feeling he'd like Laurel even if she were into talking about clothes and makeup and gossip. Weird. There was just a chemistry. A chemistry he felt so strongly.

So strongly that he'd almost kissed her tonight, in the car.

But it's a good thing you didn't, he told himself, folding his arms behind his neck. After all, nothing would be worse than if Laurel got the wrong idea and thought he was only interested in her as a hookup. That's why he'd made a point of telling her that he was psyched to have her as a friend—so she'd know he really respected her. Which he one hundred percent did.

Dylan decided that one thing was for sure as he closed his eyes. He was going to kiss Laurel on the second date. No matter *what* Cara said.

Wait a minute. He was letting Cara's advice drive him nuts. How could kissing Laurel—if he really liked her and he told her that—be such a bad move? There was no way holding himself back like this, when it felt so totally wrong, could be right. *Like earlier in the car,* he thought, stretching out his legs. He actually felt like a jerk because he *hadn't* kissed her.

Dylan's eyes popped open.

Right then and there, he decided. He'd made up his mind.

Screw it, he thought, closing his eyes, suddenly very sleepy. *I'm going to see Laurel tomorrow morning.*

And I'm going to kiss her.

The last thing Laurel wanted to do on Saturday morning was get out of bed. Which was unusual for her, considering she was a total morning person. But this morning, rising would mean exerting energy—energy she'd had sapped out of her after last night's disaster with Dylan.

Then again, she thought, rolling over onto her back, staying in bed all day would be completely pathetic.

Is that what my new life in California is going to be like? Moping about guys? First Gavin, and now Dylan.

Ugh. Laurel sat up. *I'm turning into one of those whiny girls on teen drama shows.*

There was a light knocking on Laurel's door, followed by her mother's voice. "Honey? You awake?"

Laurel sighed. Unfortunately, she was. If she were still asleep and in dreamland, she wouldn't be so miserable. "I'm up," she called. "Come in."

Ellie Bayer looked amazing for so early on a Saturday. She wore a black skirt, an unbuttoned gray silk blouse over a black tank top, and as always, her curly hair was perfectly arranged in a silver-and-turquoise barrette, with gorgeous ringlets framing her angular face.

Laurel looked down at her rumpled Ohio State Buckeyes T-shirt and her floppy shorts.

Wonderful. My mom is more of a babe than I am, she thought.

Her mom glanced down at her silver-link watch. "It's almost eleven, sweetie. I can't believe you're still in bed."

Laurel shrugged. "I was tired, I guess."

Mrs. Bayer crossed her slim arms over her chest, raising an eyebrow. Laurel noticed that she was holding a cream-colored envelope in her left hand. "Tired from your date last night?" she asked, a teasing lilt to her voice as she sat down on the edge of Laurel's bed.

Laurel's earlobes heated up. She felt like crawling under her covers and never coming out. "It wasn't a date, Mom. I told you that yesterday." *Or did you forget that along with my birthday?* she wondered. "Dylan and I are just friends."

"Oh. Okay," her mother said, the twinkle still gleaming. "But you two had fun?"

Laurel wished more than anything that her mother would just change the subject. She stared down at the swirling pattern embroidered into her comforter. "Yes."

"Well, good." She smiled. "So, your dad and I were talking about going shopping for patio furniture. Sound good to you?"

If Laurel didn't have what it took to get out of bed, there was no way she'd have the energy to stroll around store after store—especially to look at boring plastic patio furniture and ugly flowered cushions.

"I don't think I'm in the mood," Laurel mumbled.

"No?" Mrs. Bayer leaned over to brush Laurel's hair off her face. "But that way the three of us will finally get to spend some time together. Catch up. It's like we've all been leading separate lives since we moved here."

Laurel sighed. That was true. And it would be comforting to spend a day with her parents, just the three of them. But she just didn't feel like it. She didn't feel like anything. "I'll take a rain check if that's all right."

Her mom shifted closer to Laurel, leaning

forward to rest her hand on her arm. "Honey, I hope you're still not upset about your birthday. I know we only have a week to plan, but I promise we'll do something fun."

"Whatever," Laurel said. "It doesn't really matter."

Her mom's deep blue eyes widened. "Honey! Of course it matters!"

Laurel picked up Harold and fidgeted with the black stitching on his top-left paw.

Her mother shook her head, focusing on the photo of Laurel and her sisters. "*Dani*, on the other hand, let us know three years in advance that she wanted a sweet sixteen. She never stopped talking about it." She turned back to Laurel. "Oh—she got into that sorority, by the way. Delta, Delta . . . whatever. The one she liked."

Laurel smiled slightly. "Now she probably won't stop talking about *that*."

Her mother laughed. "Probably." She looked down at her lap and remembered the envelope in her hand. "Oh. I almost forgot. This just arrived in the mail."

Laurel opened the fancy envelope, noting its blue tissue lining. What was this? She pulled out a folded cream-colored invitation, which was engraved in slate gray. Very fancy. A yellow Post-it was stuck to it. Not so fancy.

Laurel, it read, *sorry for the short notice. These went out a couple of weeks before school started, and I didn't know you then! Hope you can come. Ava.*

That was nice of her, Laurel thought as she opened up the invitation. *Really nice.*

She'd been invited to Ava's sweet-sixteen party, to be held at the Pasadena Valley Country Club. The one she'd heard some girls talking about on her first day of school. Laurel smiled. This meant she *was* making friends, she realized. That was something. That was a lot, actually. Then she noted the date: next Saturday night.

Her own birthday.

Laurel stared at the fancy invitation, at the cursive script and calligraphy on the envelope. Tears stung the backs of her eyes. It wasn't that Laurel wanted a country-club party. It was . . . that Ava was having the party Laurel had described to Gavin—on her birthday, no less.

"How nice!" her mom said. "A sweet-sixteen invitation!"

"On my birthday," Laurel said, slumping down in bed. "Even if I felt comfortable inviting a few people from school over to celebrate my birthday, I couldn't. Everyone I know will be at Ava's party."

"Well, perhaps you could celebrate your birthday with your new friends at Ava's," her mom suggested. "It'll be festive."

Yeah, right, Laurel thought. She liked Ava, but celebrating someone else's birthday on her own sweet sixteen seemed . . . painful. *Am I being a brat?* Laurel wondered.

"You know, you'd probably have a great time," her mom said, caressing the engraved print. "You'd forget in half an hour that it was someone else's party. Maybe it'd even feel like your own. You'd just have to tell everyone that it's your birthday too! That way all the kids would wish you a happy birthday."

Laurel nodded. She was too overwhelmed to even speak. What else could possibly go wrong in her life?

"Sweetie, I have an idea. You can go to Ava's party on Saturday, and we'll celebrate your birthday the following weekend in high style. That'll give us time to plan something *really* wonderful. Something big. And by then you'll be more settled at school. You can even give us a list of all your new friends to invite."

Staring down at the fancy invitation, Laurel shrugged. "Okay. Sure."

Mrs. Bayer leaned over to kiss Laurel on the forehead. "Terrific." She glanced at her watch and stood up. "Dad and I aren't leaving for a while, so let us know if you change your mind and want to come."

Considering that Laurel was still in a near cata-tonic state, changing her mind was doubtful. But she nodded just the same. "Okay."

As her mom closed the door behind her, Laurel stared at the invitation in her hands. She wondered what Ava's party was going to be like.

Like a dream, she was sure. Tons of people, luxurious surroundings, great music, food, dancing. A lavish, big-deal affair.

At least she didn't have to worry about Gavin and Liza flying in to see she had no plans for her birthday. That her only invitation was to *someone else's* sweet sixteen. That would be the most humiliating thing that had happened yet.

Liza. She had to tell Liza the truth about the party—that she'd made up the whole thing to save face with Gavin. Plus she needed to talk about the Dylan fiasco. Liza would help her feel better, maybe even put things into perspective. Not that there was any perspective other than misery.

Laurel trudged over to her desk. She'd e-mail rather than call. Writing it all out would give her time to compose her thoughts, figure out how she felt about everything. Plus she might even get all her angst off her chest in the process.

She booted up and logged on. Two messages were waiting for her—one from Liza and one from Gavin. Laurel rolled her eyes. *Gavin probably wants to give me a Geena Moore update. Let me know he's officially in love and they're a major couple.*

Laurel clicked open his message. She was a regular glutton for punishment, wasn't she?

L:
   Howdy. How's it going by you?

*Guess what? Liza and I are flying out for
your birthday! We weren't sure we'd be able to,
so neither of us wanted to mention it till we had
the tickets in our hot little hands. Between our
frequent-flyer miles and, like, twelve promises
each to our parents, we were able to afford it.
One promise is that I have to visit my aunt
(she lives in LA) while I'm out there. Oh,
well. It's worth it to see you. P.S. I'm psyched
for your party! P.P.S. Things with Geena are
still going strong. You'd really like her. See you
in a week!*

—G

A wave of nausea washed over Laurel.

He's coming for my party, she thought, staring
blankly at the computer screen.

*He's coming for my nonexistent party, which I totally
bragged about.*

Laurel dropped her head in her hands, squeezing
her eyes shut. What was she going to do now?

Laurel clicked open Liza's message, barely sum-
moning the energy to push the key.

*Hi, Laurel! Guess what? Gavin and I
are flying out to California for your birthday!
He said he'd e-mail you too, so maybe you
already got his? It's too early to call you, so I
wanted to make sure you got this the minute
you wake up. We're both really excited about*

*your big bash! You'll still talk to us dull
Buckeyes, right? Can't wait to hear about
your date!*
WBS!

Love, Liza

And Laurel had thought she couldn't possibly
feel worse.

Nine

MAYBE I CAN tell Gavin and Liza *that there was a huge fire and the place that I was supposed to have my party at burned down,* Laurel thought, hugging her knees to her chest as she sat in front of her computer. *Or maybe I can tell them that I have a horrible, contagious flu and that they shouldn't come at all.*

Good idea, Laur, she berated herself. As if getting herself tangled into even bigger lies was going to help matters.

Sighing, she twirled a strand of hair around her finger. She was simply going to have to suck it up and tell them the truth.

But the mere idea of *that* made Laurel's stomach turn. She knew Liza would understand—it was Gavin she couldn't bear to come clean to.

Why was he flying out anyway? she wondered. It was such a sweet thing to do. The kind of thing the two best friends in the world would do. Laurel's heart constricted in her chest. *Gavin's coming for your birthday because he's totally dense,* she reminded herself. *Because your feelings for him didn't register at all. Or he just doesn't want to deal with it. He wants to pretend you never said any of that.*

But she had said it. And they could never go back to the way things used to be.

There was no way Laurel could tell Gavin she'd made up the party. She cringed at the thought. She'd humiliated herself enough with him. Now she was supposed to tell him she'd lied to—what? Impress him? Make him think she was over him? Act like she didn't need him in her life anymore?

"Laurel?" Her father's voice boomed out from downstairs. "Dylan's here to see you!"

Laurel's feet dropped to the floor. *Dylan? Here? Now?*

Her nerves short circuiting through her body, Laurel jumped up and opened the door a crack, peeking her head out. "Just a second!" she called. She shut the door and sat back down on her bed, frozen stiff, her heart beating at warp speed.

What was he doing here?

And why had he chosen the one morning Laurel had slept late and hadn't taken a shower or so much as brushed her hair? She glanced at the digital clock by her bed. She bit her lip. *Maybe I could take a one-minute shower?*

What was she thinking? *Dylan doesn't like you, remember?* The fact that he'd come over meant nothing. After all, this was how things had started with Gavin too. He'd constantly drop by on the spur of the moment, wanting to hang out, but only because he saw Laurel as his friend.

Friend, Laurel reminded herself. That was the operative word here. And if Dylan only liked Laurel platonically, there was no point in her worrying about how she looked. It didn't matter anyway. Clearly Dylan wasn't the least bit attracted to her.

With this resolved in her brain, Laurel let out a deep breath and pulled on her favorite blue sweatpants, then darted into the bathroom to brush her teeth and put her hair into a ponytail. *There.* She was ready to receive her new friend.

"Come on up, Dylan," she called downstairs as she sat at her desk. Her stomach was flip flopping. Why had he come over? What could he possibly want?

"Hey . . . I didn't wake you, did I?"

Her heart skipped as Dylan walked into her room. He was wearing jeans and a T-shirt, and he looked more gorgeous than ever.

Figures.

But you don't need to notice things like that, Laurel told herself. *Not unless you want to get your heart trampled.*

"Uh, no," Laurel said. "I woke up a little while ago."

"Oh." Dylan took another step inside, glancing around her room. He didn't seem to know what to do with his hands. He kept moving them around—crossing his arms and then uncrossing them, sticking them in his front pockets and then moving them around to his back pockets. . . . What was with him?

"I wish I could sleep late," he said. "I always wake up way too early."

She nodded. He was really nervous about something. But what?

Dylan's eyes fell on the photograph of Laurel with Dani and Julie. He stepped to the dresser and picked up the frame. "These your sisters?"

"Yeah," Laurel said, standing slightly behind him. "That's Julie," she explained, pointing to the taller sister with lighter hair. "She's in med school at Berkeley. And Dani's a freshman at Ohio State."

Dylan's gaze lingered on the photo. "Must be cool to have sisters. You miss them?"

"Sometimes." Laurel tried very hard not to notice Dylan's soapy, masculine smell. She took a step back, as if that would actually stop her from being attracted to him. "I always miss Julie. But I don't mind not having to fight over the bathroom with Dani anymore. The girl practically lived in there."

Dylan turned to look at her, his mouth curving into a smile, his eyes crinkling in the corners.

Laurel's pulse immediately sped up. She turned around, walking toward her window. She couldn't take this.

Why had he come over anyway? To torture her? She stared out the window, focusing on a little girl with pigtails who was riding a pink tricycle down the street, her father following a few steps behind.

"Hey. Are you okay?" he asked. "You seem kinda . . . down."

Laurel glanced back at Dylan. What could she tell him? *I really like you, so I'm depressed that you don't like me? That would go over well. Or how about: I've turned into a liar?*

She lost it. She felt the tears start, and suddenly there was no way to stop them.

I'm crying in front of Dylan, she thought in horror. *How much lower and lamer can I get?*

"Laurel?" he said, rushing over to her. "What is it? What's wrong?"

She slid down the wall onto her butt. In between sniffles she said, "Everything."

"C'mon, it can't be that bad," he told her, sitting down beside her.

"Trust me, it is," she managed to squeak. "I've got a really big problem."

"Well, that's what friends are for, right?" Dylan said, squeezing her hand. "So spill it."

Friends. That caused another sob to break loose. She never wanted to hear that word come out of a guy's mouth again.

103

She covered her face with her hands. *Get it together!* she ordered herself. *Take a deep breath and chill out!*

"Laurel?" he prodded again. "You can tell me anything. You know that, right?"

She dropped her hands and turned to face him. "I did something really stupid. So stupid, I can't even bear to correct it. And so stupid, I can't bear to tell you."

"C'mon," he said. "If you tell me, I swear I'll help you."

Laurel took a deep breath. There was no way he could help her. No one could. "Dylan, why'd you come over anyway?"

He cleared his throat. "I, um, wanted to see you."

"Why?" she asked.

"Do friends need a reason to see friends?" he replied with a sweet smile.

Laurel felt like banging her head against the wall.

"So are you gonna tell me what's eating you," he began, "or do I have to tickle it out of you?"

She laughed. Could she tell him? What if he thought she was the lamest person he'd ever met? What if he didn't even want to be her friend anymore?

"Laurel . . ."

"Okay," she said. "But don't judge me, Dylan. Promise?"

He nodded solemnly.

"I, um, was really good friends with a guy back in Ohio." Laurel stared at her toes. "And right before I moved here, I told him that I liked him *romantically*." The whole story came pouring out. She told Dylan everything, every last word, leaving out, of course, the fact that her dream date for her own nonexistent party was *him*.

Dylan raised his eyebrows. "But you're *not* having a sweet-sixteen party? Nothing?"

Laurel winced, feeling more lame than ever. Her entire face felt like it was on fire. "Well . . . no. It's just a really busy time for my parents, so they can't really plan anything. And now Gavin and Liza are coming for my birthday, expecting to go to my amazing party with all my great new friends. I'm such an idiot. I know Liza will understand when I tell her the truth, but I can't tell Gavin. I just can't."

He nodded slowly. "I see you got an invitation to Ava's shindig," he said, gesturing at the cream envelope on her desk.

Laurel glanced down. "Yeah." Tears threatened again, but she blinked them back. "Don't get me wrong—I'm really glad she invited me. It's just that . . ."

"It's the same night as your birthday," he finished for her. "That must feel pretty crummy, huh?"

Laurel crossed her arms over her chest, hugging herself. "You don't think I'm being lame for caring so much?"

Dylan shook his head. "No way. I know how it feels to want something you can't have. Something that seems in your reach, but you're powerless to make it happen."

Laurel glanced at him, surprised. "Are you talking about your mom and wanting to live with her?" She noticed he seemed a bit strained all of a sudden.

Dylan ran a hand through his hair. "Yeah. My mom and other things too."

Laurel tilted her head. "Like what?"

"Hey," he said, gently grasping her chin for a second, "we're working out your problems here, not mine. I'll tell you what—you can return the favor someday."

Laurel smiled. "Deal."

"Okay, back to this Gavin thing," Dylan said. "So you really like this guy, huh?"

Laurel froze for a second. Did she still "really like" Gavin? Or was she simply hurt and embarrassed over the way he'd treated her by throwing Geena in her face? Suddenly Laurel didn't know *how* she felt.

Well, she knew how she felt about *Dylan*.

"He really broke my heart," she admitted. "So I can't tell him the truth. I'd feel like the world's biggest loser. Plus he'd know."

"Know what?" Dylan asked, eyeing her.

"He'd know why I lied. And then things would be even more strained between us. Maybe now we have a chance to keep some semblance of a friendship. But if he knew, well, then he'd be as embarrassed I am."

Laurel leaned her head back against the wall, shocked that she was telling Dylan any of this, let alone every detail of her innermost thoughts.

"What you must think of me now," Laurel said, her voice barely above a whisper.

"Hey, I made a promise," Dylan said, looking Laurel right in the eye. "I promised I wouldn't judge you. So all I'm thinking now is that you're in a jam. Okay?"

She nodded. She looked absolutely miserable.

Gavin. Dylan wondered what the guy was like. All he knew was that he felt jealous. Jealous of anyone who'd been able to affect Laurel so much that she'd gotten herself into this kind of mess.

And jealous of the fact that Laurel was hardly over the guy. *He broke my heart. . . .*

Thank God I didn't try to kiss her last night, Dylan thought. *Or when I first got here either.* Because kissing her was exactly what he'd wanted to do the minute he arrived. The minute he saw her in her T-shirt and sweats, her hair in a ponytail.

All he'd thought about on the way over was what kissing her would feel like.

Guess I'll never know, Dylan thought, taking in Laurel's sad expression, her dark eyes so full of emotion and worry.

But even worse, Dylan hated to see Laurel so

bummed out. Somehow he'd try to snap Laurel out of this and help get her over this jerk. Which the guy had to be if he didn't feel *that way* about her.

How could any guy not feel *everything* for Laurel Bayer?

Laurel let out a sigh. "I know this all probably sounds so stupid to you. But do you understand at all? I mean, haven't you ever felt like you have to prove something to someone?"

Try all the time. Dylan's entire relationship with his father was based on Dylan proving himself. Proving that he was smart enough. Good enough. "Yeah," Dylan told her. "And I don't think it's stupid. I get it."

Laurel bit her lip, her eyes widening. "You do?"

"Yeah. But that still doesn't solve your problem, does it?"

Laurel stood up and walked over to the bed. She picked up an ancient-looking teddy bear and fidgeted with its raggedy brown ear as she dropped down on the edge. "I created this problem. I guess I'll just have to deal with it."

Dylan smiled slightly, indicating the stuffed animal with a nod of his chin. "Childhood friend?"

Laurel let out a tiny smile herself. "You could say that. Harold's been around a long time."

Dylan nodded, grinning. All right. He was getting somewhere. After all, he'd gotten Laurel to smile. That was a start. Now he just needed to figure out how he could help her.

Dylan stood up too and stared out the window. A group of little girls were playing in the front yard of the house across the street. Suddenly Dylan turned to face Laurel. He snapped his fingers. "I've got it!"

"Got what?" she asked.

Dylan walked to Laurel's desk and picked up Ava's invitation. Okay, it was a crazy idea, but who cared? It could actually work. "You've been invited to a sweet-sixteen party at the lavish Pasadena Valley Country Club on the very night of your own birthday, right?"

"Right," Laurel said, looking at him quizzically.

"And you've told your friends that you're having a lavish sweet sixteen and that all the kids from your class at Hunt are coming."

Laurel nodded.

"Not getting it yet?" he asked.

Laurel stared at him. He could tell she was thinking. "I have no idea what you're getting at."

He laughed. "You shouldn't worry about being a big-time liar, Laurel. Your mind definitely doesn't work in devious ways."

She looked at him as if he were speaking a foreign language. "Huh?"

"Tell your friend Liza the truth about the party the minute she arrives," Dylan said. "But keep Gavin in the dark. And then take Liza and

Gavin to Ava's party—which you will pretend is your *own*."

Laurel raised her eyebrows. *"What?"*

"Act like Ava's party is yours," Dylan repeated. "Gavin will never know."

Laurel laughed, a tinge of color popping out on both cheeks. "You can't be serious. That's insane."

"No, no, it's not," Dylan insisted. All right, it was, but did that really matter? In the end, who would it hurt? No one.

"No?" Laurel asked in obvious disbelief. "How am I supposed to explain two total strangers to Ava? I wasn't invited with *guests*, Dylan."

"Laurel, do you have any idea how many people are going to Ava's party?"

She shook her head.

"Try two hundred. Her family is huge, she invited the entire junior class at Hunt, and her parents invited their gazillions of 'associates.' You'll be lucky if you even *run into* Ava at the party. Trust me, if you did, she'd assume Gavin and Liza were the kids of her dad's business partners or people on her mom's charity boards."

Laurel gnawed at her lower lip. "That doesn't sound very intimate. I mean, having people you don't even know at your own birthday party?"

Dylan shrugged. "It's not something I'd be into either. But it sure does save your neck."

"Not really," Laurel said. "What about all the Happy Birthday, Ava banners? Or all those people kissing and hugging Ava, wishing her a happy birthday? How would you explain all that to Gavin?"

Dylan sat down on the bed next to Laurel. "I've been to plenty of parties at Pasadena Valley Country Club before. They don't do things like signs and decorations—they think that stuff is tacky. And there'll be *hundreds* of people there. They don't care *whose* birthday it is. They're just there for the party, for the contacts."

Laurel shook her head. "Forget it. No way."

"Trust me," he said. "It'll be easy to pull off. How hard can it be to fool one person?"

"It's too crazy, Dylan," Laurel protested. Still, as she looked down at her stuffed bear, caressing its fur, she grinned. "It's ridiculous."

Dylan shrugged. "Maybe. But what're you gonna do? Tell Gavin you lied to make him think you're having the time of your life? Tell him there is no party at all? That you have absolutely nothing planned?"

Laurel glanced up from the bear. Her eyes widened. And Dylan could tell she was wavering.

"I think you could pull it off," Dylan said.

"No way. You just said my mind didn't work in devious ways."

"Yeah, but mine does," he said. "I'll work out the details."

"I don't know. . . ."

Dylan glanced at his watch. He was late to meet

Cara for lunch. But he didn't want to go before he got a yes from Laurel. He couldn't leave her all worried. Not when his idea would take care of things for her. "Why don't we at least go to the country club tomorrow and stake the place out? My dad's a member there, so I can get us in. I'll show you how easy it'll be."

Laurel frowned. "I don't think I could. . . ."

"It's better than the alternative," Dylan argued. "Besides, when else will you get to throw a huge party for yourself for free?"

Laurel laughed. Then she turned serious. "Wait a minute, Dylan. Is this really mean to do to Ava? I mean, it's *her* party. She was nice enough to invite me, and now I'm totally going to use her party for my own needs?"

"Laurel, listen to me. Ava's cool. If you told her the story you told me, she'd tell you to do exactly what I'm telling you. She'd think it was awesome. Trust me."

She glanced down, then back up at him. He noticed a little smile tugging at her mouth. "Really?"

"Really. I know her."

She threw the stuffed bear into the air and caught it. "Okay. If you really think it'd be okay, I'll do it."

Dylan grinned. *Finally*. Those persuasive skills he'd learned from the debate team had actually gone toward something useful.

Ten

*W*HAT WAS I *thinking?* Laurel wondered as she paced around her bedroom a half hour later. She'd walked in so many anxious circles that she was starting to leave track marks in the carpet.

She stopped in place. All right, Laurel knew exactly what she'd been thinking when she'd agreed to Dylan's preposterous plan:

1. It did sort of solve her problem—if she could really pull it off;

2. That he was so charming, and so cute, and so darn persuasive, there was no possible way she *couldn't* agree to do it.

She sighed, leaning against her dresser. She didn't know which was worse. The fact that she was letting herself like Dylan or the fact that she was getting involved in yet another lie.

This is nuts, Laurel decided. A million problems popped inside her brain. What was she going to do at Ava's party—pretend that all of Ava's relatives and random friends were her own? And what about when they brought the cake and *Ava* blew out the candles? What would Laurel say then?

No. There was no way she could go through with this. She was simply going to have to call Dylan and tell him it was off.

Laurel picked up her cordless. She stared at his phone number, which he'd scrawled on a little scrap of yellow paper. But then her eyes landed on the invitation. Laurel picked up the thick paper and studied it. It definitely was an expensive-looking invitation. And from the brief description that Dylan had given of the country club, it sounded pretty swanky. Pretty classy. There'd probably be food, and drinks, and dancing. . . .

Just the kind of thing Gavin would be impressed by.

What're you gonna do? Dylan's words replayed themselves in Laurel's mind. *Tell Gavin you lied to make him think you're having the time of your life?*

She bit her lip. *That* was not an option. And as hard as it was for Laurel to believe, Dylan *had* said that it would be no problem to pull this off . . .

Laurel put down the phone.

Hmmm. Maybe this wasn't such a bad idea after all.

Half worried, half smiling, Laurel headed downstairs to tell her parents that Gavin and Liza were coming next weekend. She knew her mom and dad would be thrilled with the last minute news that her friends were coming. Her parents wouldn't have to feel so guilty about ignoring her birthday with Liza and Gavin spending the weekend.

She was *dying* to see Liza.

Gavin was another story. She had no idea what that was going to be like. But she'd soon find out.

"One small stack of blueberry granola pancakes and one cheese-and-mushroom omelette," Dave announced, placing the pancakes in front of Cara and the eggs in front of Dylan.

As usual Snazzy's, the diner where Dave worked on weekends, was packed with the brunch crowd. The sounds of silverware clattering and the constant hum of conversation and laughter filled up the long, narrow restaurant. Cara and Dylan were squeezed into a small, square table between two other overflowing tables, Cara sitting on the white faux-leather booth and Dylan in a plastic chair.

He frowned, looking down at his side of potatoes.

"I don't know, man. These hashed browns look kinda undercooked to me."

Dave narrowed his eyes at Dylan. He crossed his well-built arms over his white apron. "You send those back, and I promise you there'll be some saliva mixed in."

"Gross!" Dylan exclaimed.

Cara smiled up at her boyfriend. "My pancakes are perfect."

Dave kissed the top of her head, then sped off through the kitchen's swinging door.

Cara poured maple syrup over her pancakes. "Okay, so tell me!"

"About what?" Dylan asked, trying hard to get some stubborn ketchup out of the glass bottle. He tapped the bottle on its neck, and finally some ketchup plopped out on his potatoes. "Oh, you mean my date."

Cara rolled her eyes, which were twinkling with excitement. "C'mon! I've been waiting all morning to hear how it went! Of course, I'll get Laurel's side of the scoop later. . . ." Cara flashed him an evil grin.

"She'll tell you the same thing I'm gonna tell you," Dylan said. "We had a great time. I took her to Topper's, we oohed and ahhed at the view, and we talked a lot."

"And?"

"And nothing," Dylan said, forking a potato into his mouth. "I took her home. Took your advice too."

"Meaning you didn't try anything?"

"Nope."

"I'm very impressed, Dylan." Cara took a sip of her orange juice.

He immediately felt guilty, but only because he'd been planning to try something—until Laurel had broken down in tears in front of him this morning. He hid his guilty expression by sipping his coffee. Everything he'd just told Cara was true. There was no need to tell her he'd been about to break her advice. And there was no way he'd tell her about the plan he'd concocted for Laurel's birthday.

But there was one thing he did want Cara's advice on. He needed a girl's perspective. He hesitated, unsure if Laurel would mind him talking about it behind her back. He thought it would be okay. It wasn't like he was telling Cara for gossip's sake.

"So, Cara," he began. "I need more advice. About Laurel."

Cara took another bite of her pancakes. "What?"

"Laurel's sort of getting over a guy from Ohio." Dylan forked a piece of his omelette into his mouth. "She said he broke her heart."

Cara placed down her fork. "Really? Huh. She never mentioned it to me."

"It just came up while we were talking about that kind of thing," he said.

Cara leaned forward on the table, her hazel eyes widening. "Not good."

"Meaning?" he asked.

"Meaning I'm worried about this, Dylan. I was worried about *her* before, but now I'm worried about *you*."

Dylan's stomach turned. Why did he not like the sound of this? "What are you talking about?"

"Dylan, you don't want to be rebound guy," she stated, as if it should be perfectly obvious. "You have to take things slow."

"What? I *am* taking it slow. I already told you that."

Cara shook her head. "You don't get it. If this guy was significant, you have to take it even slower. A broken heart is significant."

Dylan blinked. *Even slower?* He didn't think that was possible. *If we took it any slower, we'd be moving in reverse.* Should he just stop talking to Laurel altogether? Forget the whole thing? Dylan leaned back in his seat, pushing away his plate of food. Why was this so insanely complicated?

At that moment Dave strolled over to the table. He took one glance at Dylan and said, "What's wrong with him?"

Cara shrugged, pushing some of her dark hair behind her ear. "Laurel's getting over a broken heart, so I was telling Dylan that he should back off a little. Give her some time before he makes his move."

At this, Dave let out a snort.

Dylan turned and glared at his friend. "What's so funny?"

Dave hooked his thumbs on the inside of his long apron, rolling forward on the balls of his feet. "Just that this is the first time I've ever seen you not able to get a girl. I find it kind of amusing, that's all."

Dylan glanced back at his uneaten, suddenly unappealing food. He'd totally lost his appetite.

At least *someone* was enjoying this.

"This place is . . . it's amazing."

Laurel's jaw dropped as she took in the arched entrance to the Pasadena Valley Country Club. She couldn't believe her eyes. A sprawling white building loomed in front of them.

Dylan put out his arm. "Shall we, madam?"

Laurel laughed and took his arm, then they strolled up the stone pathway, which was surrounded by flowers of every color.

"And this is just the entrance," Dylan said. "Wait till you see the grounds."

Laurel gasped as they reached a footbridge stretching across a pond. She glanced down at the shallow water. Bright spots of color dashed through the pond, and then Laurel saw something that made her jaw drop again. "Swans?" she exclaimed. "They actually have swans here?"

"Yep," Dylan said, following her gaze to see a

couple of the downy birds wading their way through the water. He nudged her. "At night they put on the lights. That way everyone will see the swans at *your* party."

Laurel laughed, trying hard to ignore the tingling warmth she felt as a result of Dylan's light touch. "Oh, good," she joked, glancing up at the lampposts and palm trees and weeping willows. "That's very important. Swans are essential to every party."

Dylan grinned. "This is a country club, after all."

As they continued to make their way toward the main building, Laurel took in the magnificently planted flowers and shrubs that surrounded the walkway. She felt like she was walking through some sort of enchanted garden.

"My mother would love this place," Laurel said. "Actually, I think she'd faint from excitement if she saw it."

Dylan smiled, motioning for Laurel to step inside the entranceway.

Laurel's eyes widened as she glimpsed the marble-floored front hall with extra-high ceilings. "Wow."

Dylan laughed. "I thought you'd like it."

"You know," she said, turning to face him. "I just thought of a problem. Well, one of many." A group of men and women in tennis whites were strolling by, so Laurel lowered her voice. "How are we going to explain why my own parents aren't at my sweet-sixteen party?"

"Hmmm. That will be tricky," Dylan admitted. "But not impossible. Like I told you, there will be tons of people here. We can just keep saying your parents are in the other room. Or in the kitchen, talking to the chef. Whatever—we'll figure something out."

Laurel shook her head. "Why does it seem that scheming comes so naturally to you?"

Dylan wiggled his eyebrows, his amazing green eyes sparkling. "It has to do with my very secret line of work. I'd tell you, but then I'd have to kill you."

Laurel laughed. "You make this all seem so easy. Like we'll definitely get away with this."

He looked her in the eye. "We will. Why don't you go ahead into the lobby?" he said. "I'll check us in."

"Okay." Laurel watched as he ambled over to the front desk, where a white-jacketed woman sat in front of a computer. Laurel tried very hard not to focus on how cute Dylan's butt looked in his faded jeans, but she couldn't help it.

All right, just stop, Laurel ordered herself, quickly turning around and heading off to the left toward the lobby. *He's a friend. That's all.*

As she stepped into the sunlit lobby, all thoughts of Dylan disappeared. She was too overcome by the sheer size and beauty of the room. A magnificent chandelier hung from the arched ceiling. One wall of the room was all sliding-glass doors, and the bright afternoon sunshine streamed in across the terra-cotta tiled floors and pink and beige couches and armchairs.

Off to one side was an antique banquette covered with silver tea- and coffeepots and tall glasses of ice water and iced tea, garnished with lemon slices. Perfectly accessorized men and women— some in tennis whites, others in pressed slacks and conservatively stylish skirts and dresses—were helping themselves to drinks as well as playing cards and board games, lounging around in the chairs and relaxing.

Wow, Laurel thought, playing with one of the frayed threads hanging from her old jean shorts and feeling more than self-conscious. *This is way out of my league.*

"Okay, now you've seen the lobby. Not much happens here," Dylan commented, walking up behind her.

She turned around, hugging her arms over her chest. "Why do I feel way underdressed?"

Dylan smiled. "You look great." He scanned the room, checking out the crowd. "They're the weirdos. They look so uncomfortable, don't they?"

"They do, actually," she agreed, her cheeks flushing from Dylan's offhand compliment. "So where to now?"

"Let's hit the pool," Dylan suggested. He held

out a square white sticker. "Sorry—they said you have to put this on."

Laurel took the sticker. In gold letters across the top it said Pasadena Valley Country Club. In the middle of the sticker, in bold black print, it read Guest. Laurel pulled off the sticker's backing and placed the tag on her chest. "At least I feel official. Like it's okay for me to be here."

Dylan shook his head. "You'd be okay anywhere you went, Laurel. I hate places like this. They make people feel uncomfortable, like they don't belong or they're not good enough to step on the precious fake grass. And my dad wonders why I never want to come." Running a hand through his hair, he added, "Come on. Let's go."

Laurel followed Dylan outside onto another stone pathway. He pointed across what looked like endless rolling hills. Laurel could make out a small-ish building in the distance. A white flag hung off its roof, the club's gold lettering visible on the flag's surface.

"The golf course is over there," Dylan explained. Then he pointed to the right. "And the tennis courts are that way, just around the corner." He stepped onto the path that cut across the lawn diagonally to the left. "This is the way to the pool."

Laurel followed him down the path, which was lined with pink roses and other flowers. The air was infused with their sweet scent. *Unbelievable.*

123

This place was straight out of a movie. The country club back in Grange, consisting of a run-down clubhouse, half of a golf course, and an indoor pool that always reeked of chemicals and chlorine, was *nothing* like this.

Laurel smiled to herself. Gavin was going to lose it when he saw this place.

As they reached the pool, Laurel almost lost it herself. People lounged by the huge, kidney-shaped pool and in the Jacuzzi. Two young men in crisp white shorts and collared shirts emblazoned with the country club's gold insignia carried trays of Evian and washcloths, passing them out to guests.

"Washcloths?" Laurel said, watching as one of the men stopped to hand a towel to a woman in a red bathing suit.

"They're cold. That way you don't have to sweat while you're tanning," Dylan explained, shaking his head.

Laurel continued to watch the woman as she delicately patted her flushed face and chest with the towel. "That's too much."

"No kidding. And check out the jewelry these women are wearing to go with their bikinis."

Laurel glanced around, noticing that the majority of women wore the works: necklaces and bracelets and rings and earrings. Lots of gold and diamonds.

124

"What?" Laurel said mockingly. "I *always* wear my diamonds to the pool."

Dylan grinned, that cleft in his chin deepening. "Yeah. I figured that about you." He stuck his hands in pockets. "Should we continue with our tour?"

"Let's continue," she agreed. "I'll come pat my face with a washcloth later."

Dylan laughed. "By the way, this is where the cocktail hour will be. They light up the pool, take away the lounge chairs, and serve food and drinks out here."

"Sounds really nice," she said, imagining how that would look. Special. Romantic. She followed Dylan to a gazebolike shelter at the head of the pool. Underneath it was a circular bar, which was surrounded by tables and chairs. She envisioned sipping an iced tea out here while gazing at Dylan under the moonlight. . . .

They reached another building. Dylan pulled open the doors' gold handles. "And this is where the party will be."

Laurel felt a refreshing blast of cool air as soon as she stepped inside. The room had that brand-new lemony scent, kind of like a hotel. Hugging her arms to keep warm, Laurel glanced around the enormous, empty space.

Multiple glass chandeliers hung from the ceiling—miniversions of the one in the lobby—and the floor was lined with deep burgundy carpeting, accented with tiny specks of gold. In the center of the room was a dance floor.

"There will be hundreds of people here. Guaranteed," Dylan explained. "And there won't be any Ava signs or decorations." He crossed the dance floor and sat down on the stage. "This is where the band will be." He shrugged. "That's all. Very straightforward. It'll be easy."

Laurel arched an eyebrow. "Easy, huh?" She sat down next to him. "And what am I going to do when they bring out Ava's cake and the band decides to sing happy birthday?"

Dylan smiled. "You're not going to stump me. I'll just get Gavin out of the room the second I see them bringing out the cake. No problem."

"Right." Laurel laughed. "No problem." Twirling a strand of hair around her finger, she looked around the room, trying to imagine it filled with people and music and food. "It does sound like it'll be incredible," she added. "The funny thing is, if I was going to have a sweet sixteen, I wouldn't have a party this . . . lavish." She glanced at Dylan. "Not that it would be an option for me, of course. But even it was, I'd feel more comfortable with something a little more low-key . . . a bonfire on the beach with my close friends, maybe. Yeah. That's what I would want."

Dylan nodded. "I'm with you. A bonfire on the beach sounds great."

Laurel searched Dylan's face for a moment.

She had a question, but she wasn't sure she wanted to ask.

Because you know what the answer will be.

"Dylan? Why are you doing this? I mean, why are you going to all this trouble? You can back out, you know. I'll understand."

She knew what he was going to say. *Because you're my friend . . .*

Dylan looked at her silently for a moment. Then he glanced down, fidgeting with his silver ring. "It's no trouble," he said finally. "Really. Look, this guy hurt you, right?"

Laurel nodded. *You could definitely say that.*

"Okay. Here's the thing," Dylan said. "Lying will always get you into trouble. You know that, right? I mean, this whole situation is the perfect example."

She nodded. "Definitely."

"So you've already learned whatever cosmic lesson you're supposed to," Dylan pointed out. "If I can help you out of it, why shouldn't I? After what you've been through with this guy, why should you have to feel one more second of heartache?"

Laurel was so touched that she couldn't speak. She could only stare into his incredible green eyes. "I guess. . . ."

"Hey, you're cold." Dylan glanced down at Laurel's goose-bump-lined skin. He put both hands against her arms, rubbing them up and down, trying to warm her up. "Maybe we should get out of here."

At his touch, tingles shot from the top of her skull to the bottom of her toes. Her heart thumping against her rib cage, Laurel imagined herself kissing Dylan.

Was it her imagination, or was he leaning closer to her?

He was.

No. He wasn't. Laurel turned away, pushing a strand of hair behind her ear. *Stop pretending that he wants to kiss you,* she thought, grasping onto the edge of the stage. *You'll only get hurt.*

Laurel jumped up. "Thanks, Dylan. For everything."

He smiled. "No problem."

Yeah, she thought. *No problem. Except for the fact that I'm totally into you.*

Eleven

LAUREL WAS GORGEOUS, there was no doubt about that. But getting her beauty down on paper was another matter altogether.

Leaning back in his desk chair on Sunday evening, Dylan squinted and held his charcoal sketch of Laurel at arm's length, trying to figure out what he was missing. The drawing resembled her a little bit, but something was definitely off.

That deep, triangular indentation above her top lip, Dylan realized. It was so sexy. He'd noticed it today when they were sitting in the country club's ballroom. When it would have been so easy to lean over and kiss her.

He put the sketch paper back down on his desk under the bright light of his brass lamp and erased the lines around Laurel's upper lip.

Man. He'd spent a lot of time looking at that lip

today. And those eyes. And those *legs* . . .

Dylan shook his head, dropping the flat pink eraser. He picked up the small porcelain Buddha off his desk, the one his mother had bought him in China, and rolled it in his hands.

He had come so close to kissing Laurel today. He'd been about to . . . when she moved away—abruptly. Obviously Cara was right. When a girl was getting over a broken heart, another guy would be rebound material. Nothing more. Laurel was *clearly* not over Gavin. Dylan could totally lose her if he pushed things too fast.

He sighed, putting down the Buddha. *Looks like I've got to be patient,* he thought, picking up the piece of charcoal. Unfortunately, Dylan Fraiser wasn't exactly known for his patience. If he wanted something, he wanted it *now*.

"Dylan? What are you doing?"

Dylan swiveled around; his father stood in the doorway to his bedroom, a scowl on his face.

"You've been running around all day," his dad said. "Shouldn't you be doing something more productive? Don't you have homework?"

Dylan glanced down. Was his father's sole purpose in life to nag him? "I'm on top of it, Dad. Don't worry about it."

"You're on top of it, huh?" Stephen Fraiser shook his head. "We'll see about that when we get your grades. Just make sure everything's done, all right?"

As if Dylan didn't always do that anyway. "Yeah. Okay," Dylan mumbled.

"All right. 'Night, Dylan. Don't stay up too late." Then he was gone.

Sighing, Dylan stood up and shut the door. *Guess my art doesn't fall under the category of "productive,"* Dylan thought, trudging back to his desk. He glanced at his laptop. He had an idea of something *productive* he could do.

He logged on to the Internet, congratulating himself on his brilliance. After addressing a group e-mail to everyone in his address book, he typed:

> *Hey, there. Just wanted you all to know that Saturday is Laurel Bayer's birthday.*

Smiling to himself, Dylan hit the send button. Now everybody would wish Laurel a happy birthday at Ava's party—in front of Gavin.

Sometimes Dylan was so good, he scared himself. He pulled a piece of scrap paper from his pocket: Laurel's e-mail address. Composing a new message, this one addressed to Laurel, he typed:

> *Laurel,*
> *Had fun hanging out with you today. Want to come over Thursday night? To go over some last minute details?*

He hit send, then stretched out his legs, leaning back in his upholstered chair.

Hey. If that hadn't been productive, he didn't know what was.

"I wish you had come with us today," Laurel's mother said, placing a basket of rolls on the table.

Laurel's father nodded, digging into his linguine with clams. "We ended up driving to a store in Santa Monica and decided to have lunch there. It's kind of a tourist trap, but walking along the pier is a lot of fun. We'll go another time."

"Actually, I sort of saw it the other night. The restaurant that Dylan and I went to was in Santa Monica," Laurel told her parents, reaching to take a sip of water. "It had great views of the beach."

"Really?" Laurel's father asked. "Maybe we can all go sometime. So, Laurel, this Dylan seems like a nice guy."

"I'll bet he's really cute too," Laurel's mother added, resting her chin in her hands.

Laurel's earlobes burned. She knew that gleam in her mother's blue eyes. It was the you-finally-have-a-boyfriend gleam. It was bad enough that Laurel had to deal with her own heart-crushing disappointment in terms of Dylan. The last thing she wanted was to have her parents' expectations piled on top of it.

"I already told you, Mom, he's just a friend."

Laurel pushed her linguine around in her white-sunflower-trimmed bowl.

"Oh. Right. I know." Her mom waved off Laurel's discomfort with a gesture of her hand. "But it is sweet of him to show you around." She speared a cherry tomato with her fork. "He took you to the country club today?"

"Yes," Laurel said, dying to get off the subject of Dylan. Because when she thought about him, she thought about how much she liked him . . . and how much she had wanted to kiss him today. . . . She glanced down at her lap, her heart sinking. And how that was *never* going to happen.

"What's the club like?" Laurel's father asked. "Is it very swanky?"

"Totally."

Laurel's mom tilted her head, eyeing Laurel's dad. "Hmmm, maybe we should check it out, hon."

Laurel sat forward, taking another bite of her pasta. "It wasn't exactly my speed, but it's the kind of place you and Dani would love."

"Uh-huh." Laurel's mother smiled. "In other words, you hated it."

Laurel smiled as well, twirling another bite onto her fork. "I didn't *hate* it. It was just a little . . . over-done." She hadn't meant to be mean.

"Mmm-hmm. And this club is where Ava's party is going to be?" Laurel's mother asked.

Yeah. And my imaginary party, Laurel thought, her earlobes heating up once again. "Right."

"I'll bet you have a wonderful time at Ava's party, Laur," her dad said. "Your mom and I had some ideas about what we could do for your birthday—the following Saturday, maybe?"

"Actually *Julie* had an idea," Laurel's mother added. "We spoke to her today, and she suggested we rent out a room in a nice restaurant. You could invite a big group of friends."

Laurel shifted in her seat. The idea of planning a *real* sweet sixteen in addition to the faux party that she was already plotting suddenly seemed very wrong. She felt guilty enough.

Laurel placed down her fork, looking from her mother to her father. "You know what? I know I made a big deal about wanting to celebrate my birthday and everything, but I really don't care."

Laurel's parents exchanged a wary look.

"Really," she insisted. "Let's just forget about it."

"Honey," Laurel's mother protested. "We don't want to *forget* about your birthday."

"Not my birthday, just the party," Laurel explained. "Besides, Liza and Gavin are coming *this* weekend. I wouldn't want to have a party next Saturday with them not here. And anyway," Laurel went on, reaching with her fork for one last mouthful of linguine, "Gavin and Liza being here will be celebration enough."

Laurel's father shook his head, his brown eyes uncertain. "If you say so . . ."

"I say so," Laurel assured him. "But thanks. I

mean, I really appreciate it. I'll definitely call Julie and thank her for thinking of it."

If following through with the stupidest plan in history wasn't enough of an activity for her birthday, Laurel didn't know what was.

On Tuesday evening Laurel sat on Cara's bedroom floor, her French textbook open on the floor beside her. She and Cara were working on their oral presentation. The project was on a movie they'd seen last week, *Le Grand Chemin*. Laurel was a good enough student herself, but being teamed up with Cara ensured a very good grade.

"I started doing some background notes last night," Cara said. She pulled open her desk drawer and took out a rubber-banded pack of multicolored index cards. Tossing the cards over to Laurel, she explained, "The pink cards are about character issues, the blue about plot, and the green are my notes on themes."

Laurel raised her eyebrows as she slipped off the rubber band and read the back of the first card—a pink one. "This is amazing!"

Cara smiled and sat at her desk. "Dave teases me about how organized I am. But I can't function any other way. Dave can ace a test without even studying."

"Really?" Laurel put the rubber band back over the cards. "That must be so annoying."

"It is." Cara laughed. "We're much better off

when we *don't* have classes together."

Laurel laughed too. Her eyes fell on a photo of Cara and Dave that sat on Cara's desk, next to her computer. They looked so happy. Laurel stared at the photo wistfully. "How long have you guys been going out?"

Cara smiled. "Since freshman year. I can't even believe it."

"*I* can." Laurel tossed the index cards onto the plush carpeting. "I could see you guys getting married."

"Whoa." Cara held up one hand as if she were halting traffic. "First we gotta see if we make it through the rest of high school, let alone college." Picking up the cards, she shook her head. "Marriage is a long way off."

Laurel smiled. "I know. Just fantasizing a little, I guess."

Cara ran her hand over the edge of the cards, giving Laurel a mischievous look. "Don't go telling Dave that. Gotta keep the guy guessing, you know."

Laurel smiled. "Understood."

Cara laughed and glanced down at the cards. She started to pull off the rubber band, then hesitated, regarding Laurel carefully—as if a thought had just popped into her brain. "So, um, Dylan mentioned to me that you're getting over someone back in Ohio. He wasn't telling me in a gossipy way or anything."

Laurel's hand flew up to her hair, twisting a strand around her finger. "Basically, I got my heart totaled."

"That must be hard," Cara said, her eyebrows scrunching together, her tone soft with concern. "Especially with him being so far away."

Laurel stared down at her beat-up old sneakers. "It is."

Cara nodded, her expression sympathetic. "Listen, I just have to tell you this one thing."

"What?" Laurel asked, more than a little curious.

"Okay. I hate to butt in. But I just want you to know that Dylan is a really, really great guy," Cara began, sending Laurel's heart racing. Where was she going with this?

Cara stood, shaking her head. "Dylan would kill me if he knew I was saying anything to you." She started to walk in circles in front of a thoroughly confused Laurel. "But it's just that, well, I know that Dylan has kind of been a player in the past. And I know that you're probably nervous about getting hurt after what just happened with the guy back in Ohio. But Dylan would really make *someone* an incredible boyfriend." Cara paused, stopping in place and focusing back on Laurel. "So just keep an open mind about him. Okay?"

Laurel blinked. Cara's words all blended together in an incomprehensible haze. *He's a great guy . . . been a player . . . incredible boyfriend.*

Wait a minute. Was it Laurel's imagination, or was Cara *encouraging* Laurel to go out with Dylan? Her heart pounded in her ears and her palms began to sweat as utter confusion swirled around in her brain.

Laurel realized that there were two distinct possibilities here. Either Cara was taking it upon herself to set up Laurel and Dylan, or Dylan had said something about Laurel to Cara.

Laurel's heart swelled.

But then it deflated. Who was she kidding? Cara liked Laurel, and she liked Dylan. The girl was simply telling Laurel that Dylan wasn't necessarily the player he was rumored to be—for the *right* girl. A girl he liked. Cara probably didn't know that Dylan had already made it clear that he only liked Laurel as a friend.

"Sure," she told Cara, trying to make her voice sound steady. "Okay."

Cara broke into a grin. She dropped down and gave Laurel a quick hug. "I could see you two together—especially since you guys are like the king and queen of varsity soccer! Hey—I forgot to congratulate you on making the team. Good going!"

Good going.

If Cara only knew.

Twelve

"YOU'VE THOUGHT OF everything, haven't you?" Laurel asked as she sat on the edge of Dylan's bed on Thursday night. "You've really thought this whole thing through."

Dylan shrugged from his perch on top of his desk. He tried to appear nonchalant. For the past ten minutes he'd been going over the details of how they were going to pull off this whole party thing. And Laurel was right. He *had* thought this whole thing through. But that was only because he basically spent every waking moment thinking about Laurel. Naturally, the party became intertwined in those thoughts.

Still, Dylan didn't think it would be the suavest move to let Laurel know that. "You've got nothing to worry about."

"You definitely make it sound that way." Laurel

smiled, and that cute dimple popped out on her left cheek. As usual, Laurel looked gorgeous tonight. And also as usual, it didn't take much to make her look gorgeous. She wore jeans and a pale purple, V-necked T-shirt that did an excellent job of accentuating her dark hair and eyes.

"One more thing," Dylan said, hopping off his desk. He lifted a square card from his desk and handed it to Laurel. "So you can show it to your friends."

Laurel's dark brown eyes widened the moment she took the card in her hands. "Dylan. This is incredible."

"It's nothing." Dylan sat down on the bed next to her, glimpsing his artwork from over Laurel's shoulder. The card was a fake invitation to Laurel's sweet sixteen. The block lettering he'd carefully printed in gray ink actually looked decent, and the purple border—a mixture of birthday candles and abstract festive designs—appeared somewhat professional.

"No. It's perfect," Laurel argued, running her finger around the smooth border of the card. "And purple is my favorite color."

"Yeah. I know," Dylan responded.

Laurel immediately glanced up at him, obviously surprised.

Dylan cleared his throat. "I mean, I figured," he amended. He scratched the back of his neck, motioning to Laurel's purple shirt with his eyes. "You kind of wear it a lot."

Laurel's cheeks flushed. "Oh yeah. I guess I do." She focused back on the card, shaking her head. "So what did you do? Have someone draw this?"

"I did it."

Laurel blinked, dropping the card down in her lap. "*You* drew it? You drew *this*?"

Dylan felt sheepish. "Yeah. I told you. It's nothing."

Laurel stood, grasping the invitation in her hand. "*This* is not nothing, Dylan." She pointed at him with the card. "I mean, this is really good."

Dylan smiled. "Thanks." It felt so good to have someone compliment his work.

"I didn't know you were an artist," she said.

Dylan shrugged. "I wouldn't say *that*. I like drawing and painting, that's all."

"And you're very good at it," Laurel told him. She took a moment to glance around, her eyes scanning Dylan's walls, taking in the photographic posters from around the world. "Can I see some of your work?"

His sketch of Laurel was sitting in his bottom desk drawer. But there was no way he'd show her *that*. It would most definitely weird her out.

Still, Dylan did have a sketch pad filled with work he'd done in Israel. He felt good enough about most of those drawings to show them to someone.

He picked up his large, black sketchbook.

"You could look through these if you want."

Laurel took the sketchbook and sat back down on his bed. She opened it, mesmerized by the first drawing.

Dylan stood next to her, shifting his weight from one foot to the other and not having a clue what to do with his hands—moving them from pocket to pocket, folding them over his chest, then unfolding them. He was nervous. Anxious. Normally he didn't care what anyone else thought about his work. Well, anyone except for his teachers. Swallowing, Dylan stretched his arms in front of him, cracking his knuckles. But he definitely cared what Laurel thought. A lot.

She shook her head slightly, her mouth dropping open as she turned a page. "Dylan," she whispered, gazing at a drawing. "These are amazing."

"Yeah?" Dylan asked, sitting down next to her. "You think so?"

"Are you kidding?" Laurel turned to look at him, a smile lighting up her face. "Definitely." Her eyes fell back on the picture of an old man with a long, white beard sitting with a little boy on a beach.

"Come on." Laurel nudged Dylan with her elbow. "You have to know how good you are."

Dylan grinned. He ran a hand though his wavy blond hair. "I'm *okay*."

"Okay?" Laurel laughed, rolling her eyes.

"Please." She flipped the page, turning to an unfinished sketch of a group of Bedouin in the middle of the Israeli desert. "Wow," she murmured, shaking her head. "I can't believe I didn't know this about you." She turned the page once more, this time revealing a drawing of a mosque. "What art classes are you taking at school?"

Dylan let out a frustrated laugh. "None."

"None?" Laurel glanced up from Dylan's sketch pad. "Why not?"

Dylan sighed. He scooted back on his bed so that he was leaning against the wall. "The class I wanted to take meets the same time as debate."

Laurel placed the book down on the gray comforter and turned to face Dylan. Her dark eyebrows furrowed together. "And debate is very important to you?"

Dylan shook his head. "To my dad."

Laurel frowned. "Well, then, there's no problem." She moved closer to Dylan. "Your *dad* can take debate. You can take the art class."

Dylan's mouth formed into a half smile. If only it was that easy. "My father would never go for it. He thinks I need things like debate to get me into college." Dylan glanced down. "And he thinks art is basically a waste of time. That it'll never get me anywhere."

Laurel let out a gasp. "But that isn't true."

Dylan smiled at her.

Laurel moved even closer. "My father works

143

at a university, and I know for a fact that excelling at something like art or music definitely makes you stand out when you apply to college. Do you know how many debate-club members or class presidents these admission officers see? And second, anything that you love doing—not to mention are extremely talented at—is never a waste of time."

She paused, letting out a quick breath. "*And* there are lots of things you can do with art besides being a straight-out artist. My mom was a design major, and she started out her career in advertising. Now she works for an art Web site. Art is very important. It gives pleasure to lots of people. And if I were as talented as you, I would be drawing and painting—not arguing with the debate team."

Dylan crossed his arms over his chest, amused. "Tell that to my dad."

Laurel winced slightly, pushing a strand of hair behind her ear. "Does he bite?"

"A little." Dylan stretched his legs out in front of him, grinning. "You're absolutely right, though." He put down the pillow. "Problem is, that doesn't get me anywhere. *I* know you're right, but my dad will never agree."

"So? *Make him* agree," Laurel argued.

Dylan raised his eyebrows, surprised by the forcefulness of Laurel's tone.

She shrank back a little, her eyes wide. "Okay.

144

Maybe it's not my business or anything. But you're sixteen—you should be able to choose your classes. And you should definitely be allowed, and encouraged, to do something that's obviously very important to you."

Dylan suddenly felt like a total wimp. Laurel had a point. It was time that he stood up to his father already.

Laurel leaned forward, lightly touching Dylan's arm. "In two years you'll be in college," she went on, her voice softer. "And then your dad's not going to be able to tell you what classes to take. He might as well get used to it now."

Dylan glanced up, meeting Laurel's unwavering gaze. *Man*. She was so totally right. *She's so beautiful,* he thought, taking in the way her glossy dark hair framed her angular face . . . the way her large, shimmering eyes were pleading with him. . . .

Dylan swallowed. She was so right about everything.

And so completely right for him.

His heart slamming against his chest, Dylan moved closer to her. Suddenly all he could think about was kissing her. All he *wanted* to do was kiss her. He moved closer . . . and closer . . . tipping his head toward her full lips. . . .

Then Laurel blinked.

Dylan drew back slightly as he noticed a look of wariness cross Laurel's face. Her large, dark eyes appeared tentative. Unsure.

In a flash Dylan remembered the way Laurel had pulled away from him at the country club the other day. *It's too soon,* Dylan realized. Laurel didn't want this. And he was on the verge of screwing up everything that had developed between them if he didn't control himself.

Dylan whispered into her ear, "Thank you." Then he pulled back.

Laurel's eyes darkened. She looked hurt. The whisper into her ear hadn't fooled her. She knew he'd been about to kiss her. *Hurt that I'd try to kiss her,* Dylan thought, swallowing. *Hurt that I'm trying to rush things.*

Man. The back of Dylan's neck began to sweat. He had to say *something.* Something that would make Laurel realize that everything was okay between them. That he'd slow it down.

"Thanks," he mumbled finally, his face heating up at his own awkwardness. "You're really . . . a great friend."

Laurel's face fell, and Dylan's stomach twisted into a tight knot.

Way to go, Fraiser, he thought. *Way to be articulate.*

Thirteen

*D*ON'T CRY. DO not *cry*.

The *f* word had the power to start her sobbing. Laurel's heart definitely felt like it was going to explode. But one thing was perfectly clear as she glanced at Dylan. She couldn't cry in front of him now. Which meant she had to get away from him immediately. And go home. And cry.

For a moment she'd actually thought he might kiss her. He'd leaned so close. And she'd been so surprised. But he'd only meant to sweetly whisper a thanks in her ear. She was just a pal to him. That was all she'd ever be.

She scooted off Dylan's bed, glancing down to look at her watch . . . which she wasn't wearing today. "Uh, I gotta go," she said, her cheeks flushing red. She grabbed her sneakers and stuffed her feet into them.

Dylan moved off the bed. *"Now?"*

"Yeah. I told my mom I'd, um, go somewhere with her," Laurel managed lamely, her knees feeling weak. She rushed toward the door. "So, bye. See you tomorrow."

"Wait." Dylan picked up the faux invitation and handed it to Laurel. "Don't forget this."

"Right. Thanks." Laurel stared at the card, feeling the tears threatening to surface. "And thanks for everything else. Bye." Before she broke down altogether, Laurel turned to go, starting down the wooden staircase.

"Hold up. I'll show you out," Dylan called from behind her.

But Laurel waved him off without turning around. "That's okay," she called back, practically out the front door.

It really was a miracle that Laurel found her way home from Dylan's house. It was about a fifteen-minute walk, and she was still learning the roads of Pasadena. Not to mention that she was so upset, she could barely focus, let alone concentrate on where she was going. Thankfully, it was still light out, and Laurel was at her house before she knew it—even if she wasn't quite sure how she'd gotten there.

"I'm home!" she yelled as she opened the front door. Then she ran up to her room and closed the door behind her. She flopped onto her four-poster bed, one thought occupying her brain.

How could I let this happen again? she wondered miserably. She sniffled, a single tear making its way down her cheek. Somehow, even though she'd told herself again and again that it wasn't possible, *somehow* Laurel had let herself believe that Dylan was actually interested in her. *I set myself up for this,* she realized, tasting salt as the tear ran over her lips. *How stupid can I be?*

Laurel rubbed her eyes, trying to stop the tears from flowing. After all her experiences, one thing was now perfectly obvious.

Love was not in the cards for her.

Dylan couldn't believe it.

That whole weird scenario in his bedroom, which he didn't even know how to describe, had now translated into Laurel being completely cold to him.

At first, when Dylan passed Laurel in the hall after homeroom on Friday morning and she barely said hello to him, he wrote it off. She was tired, maybe. In a hurry. It was possible she didn't even see him. But he'd bumped into her two more times after that, and at each encounter Laurel had given Dylan the same distant, barely audible, non-eye-contact greeting.

And for what? Okay, Dylan understood that he'd messed up by going in for a kiss when he knew full well that she was getting over some guy. A guy she was going to an awful lot of trouble to impress tomorrow night. But angry? How could Laurel be mad at him for being attracted to her? Especially when it was physically impossible not to be.

Sighing, Dylan navigated his way around the lunch line in the cafeteria, nodding in response to the seventeen *hi, Dylans* and stopping only to reach over a short, red-haired freshman and grab a peanut-butter-and-jelly sandwich. Since Dylan's nerves were so jangled, he wasn't exactly hungry. A sandwich was probably all he needed for lunch.

Breaking free of the line, Dylan stepped off to the side and scanned the sunshine-filled room, looking for Cara and Dave. Maybe Laurel would actually speak to him if she was forced to sit next to him for forty-five minutes.

But when Dylan finally spotted Cara and Dave at a corner table next to the large window overlooking Hunt's grassy quad, Laurel was nowhere in sight. *Great,* he thought, tugging on the neckline of his forest green T-shirt. *She's probably avoiding me or something.* He ambled over to Cara and Dave's table, his broad shoulders slumping.

"Where's Laurel?" he asked his friends, tossing his sandwich onto the square tabletop and dropping down into an orange chair.

Dave leaned back, crossing his arms over his chest. "Hey, how ya doing, Dylan? Nice to see you too."

Dylan rolled his eyes. "I'm sorry, all right?" A guilt trip wasn't something he needed right now. "I'm not in that great a mood today."

"I don't think Laurel is either," Cara commented, snapping off a piece of her crunchy taco.

Dylan turned to look at Cara. Wait a minute. Maybe this was all in his head. Maybe Laurel wasn't mad at him at all. It could be that something else was going on with her and Dylan was just being paranoid. "Has she been cold to you too?"

Cara sat forward, resting her chin in the palm of her hand. "Not cold. Just . . . weird. Quiet. She bailed out on lunch because she said she needed to meet with a teacher."

Dylan thought about this as he unwrapped the plastic on his sandwich. He'd be relieved if Laurel's strange mood had nothing to do with him, but he still didn't like the idea of her being bummed out. "Wonder what's wrong with her."

"Actually, I think I know," Cara told him. She broke off another piece of her taco. "It's not that hard to figure out. Didn't she say that guy is coming to visit this weekend?"

Dylan nodded. "Gavin. So?"

"*So?*" Cara rolled her eyes. "Dylan, her feelings aren't resolved about the guy. She's probably freaked out about seeing him."

Dylan put his sandwich back on the table, his stomach twisting. He'd forgotten the reason Laurel was going to all this trouble: *Gavin.* But at least

151

she wasn't behaving weirdly because she was mad at Dylan. He picked up the plastic that his sandwich had been wrapped in and wadded it up into a ball. Not that *that* was good news either. That Laurel was pining away for Gavin, planning this whole charade for him, wasn't a pleasant thought. Basically, it sucked.

Dylan sighed, tossing the plastic ball across the table. This whole situation couldn't possibly be more complicated.

"What's the deal anyway, man?" Dave suddenly asked, taking a sip of his neon orange punch. "Why haven't you hooked up with her yet?"

Cara glared at her boyfriend. "*Because.* He respects her. And he's taking it slow."

Dave's mouth formed into a lopsided grin as he shook his head. "I don't know about that. I think you're losing your touch, Fraiser." Dave reached over, slapping Dylan across the back. "And I, for one, am disappointed."

Make that two, Dylan thought, staring down at the table and at his barely eaten lunch.

Because if Dylan was anything, he was most definitely disappointed.

Laurel knew this whole situation was her fault. She really did. But on Friday afternoon at soccer practice, it helped to blame Dylan for her heartbreak too. And it especially helped to pretend that the black-and-white leather ball was

Dylan's head. Releasing all of her anger, hurt, and frustration in one fell swoop as she whaled the soccer ball into the goal had to be therapeutic. It just had to be.

Laurel stood in place, her heart hammering inside her chest and sweat pouring down her forehead as she watched her shot sail right past Amy and into the left corner of the goal.

"Way to go! You are an animal today!" Ava exclaimed from behind Laurel.

Laurel shot Ava a weak smile, which was all she could manage. "Ava, um, can I talk to you for a minute?"

"Sure, what's up?" Ava said, tightening her ponytail.

"I feel really bad about asking this," Laurel started, "especially because you were nice enough to invite me as it is, but, um, my two best friends from Ohio are flying in to visit me for the weekend since it's my birthday tomorrow, and, um—"

"Ooh—happy birthday in advance!" Ava exclaimed. "And you want to know if it's okay to bring your friends to my party, right?"

Laurel swallowed and waited.

"Of course it's okay!" Ava said. "There are gonna be so many strangers there, I wouldn't have known the difference! The party is more for my parents than for me anyway. My birthday was two weeks ago, but the country club was booked, so . . .

I am psyched for the party, though. It's gonna be so much fun."

Laurel smiled. Whew. So at least she'd cleared bringing Liza and Gavin with Ava. That was a relief.

"Girls!" the coach shouted. "Less talking, more kicking!"

Laurel moved out of the way so Ava could take her shot. *An animal. Huh.* That was one way to describe Laurel's current emotional state.

Every time she looked at Ava, she worried about what she was doing tomorrow night. Nothing about tomorrow was right. She was making a mockery of Ava's kindness in inviting her to her party. She still hadn't told Liza the truth about tomorrow, and Liza and Gavin were probably on the plane to California right now. They were due in tonight at seven-thirty.

And on top of everything, she was nothing more to the guy she was crazy about than The Friend. Maybe someone was getting Laurel back for the lies she'd told. For the big hoax she was going to attempt to pull off tomorrow night. Scammers and liars didn't deserve to be happy. That had to be it.

Weird. Laurel was so pent up about Dylan that she hadn't even registered the fact that she'd be seeing Gavin in mere hours. She wasn't all tied up in knots over it, like she thought she'd be. Or maybe she was and just couldn't separate her emotions anymore. She had a hundred and one things to be miserable about.

Water. Laurel needed water. Actually, she needed a lot of things, but a sip of water would certainly be a good start. Pulling at her gray, sweat-soaked T-shirt, Laurel headed toward the metal fountain at the corner of the field without bothering to ask her coach for permission. At the moment Laurel didn't care what her coach thought. She didn't care what anyone thought. She just wanted to go home and hide in bed.

No, Laurel thought as she reached the fountain. *Stop thinking like that.* She bent down to take a sip, pushing some loose, damp strands of hair behind her ear. *You sound pathetic. And whiny. And—*

"Hot today, huh?"

Laurel's nerves partied in her stomach at the sound of Dylan's voice. She let go of the fountain's lever, stopping the lukewarm water from flowing. Slowly Laurel straightened and faced Dylan. Darn. Why did he have to look so good, his deep-set green eyes so full of energy and warmth, his thick, wavy hair so—

"Yeah," she said quietly, kicking at a twig. "It is."

A heavy silence fell between them. Laurel knew that she should tell Dylan she had to get back to practice, but for some reason she couldn't get herself to move. Her feet were rooted on the spot, her eyes focused on the ground.

"So. You going to Gracie's for pizza after practice?" Dylan asked, breaking the silence.

Laurel's neck and shoulders stiffened. A lot of good that would do her—spending even more time with Dylan. Laurel shook her head, wrapping several strands of hair around her finger. "No. Can't," she mumbled.

Dylan's eyes clouded over. "Laurel? Can I ask you something?"

Laurel knew that she shouldn't look up and into Dylan's eyes. But he sounded so sincere. So concerned. "What?"

"Are you okay?" Dylan's forehead creased into tiny lines. "I mean, is something wrong?"

What a joke. Dylan wanted to know what was wrong. If Laurel wasn't so unhappy, she might have even laughed. But right now, laughing was the last thing she felt like doing.

"No," she said finally. "Nothing's wrong."

Dylan stared at Laurel, looking her over as if he didn't quite believe her. Shifting his weight from one foot to the other, he opened his mouth, clearly about to say something, but then closed it.

"I should get back," Laurel told him, tilting her head toward the area of the field where the girls were practicing. She took a step away.

"Laurel . . . wait," Dylan called after her.

Stopping in place, Laurel closed her eyes. Why didn't he get it? Why didn't Dylan understand that it was too painful for her to be around him? She turned around.

Dylan scratched the back of his neck. "Oh, uh, nothing," he said. "Just that, well, I guess we've settled everything for the party tomorrow. So . . . I'll see you there?"

Laurel felt a wave of nausea wash over her at the mere mention of the party. So far, planning the stupid thing had only brought her misery. And the actual event was sure to be a disaster. Laurel couldn't believe she was actually going through with such a ridiculous lie.

"Yeah," she told him. "Guess so." For a second she worried that she was being cold to him, but then she realized he probably wouldn't even notice it. She was just a friend to him, like Cara and Dave. He'd asked her if everything was okay, she said yes, and that was that. Nuances of her moods weren't going to register with a guy who only saw her as a buddy.

Laurel swallowed and turned around, walking away from Dylan as fast as she could. The more distance she put between them, the better.

Laurel sighed. Too bad that distance did absolutely nothing to make her stop liking him.

Who in the world does she think she is? Dylan thought, gripping his steering wheel tightly as he drove home from soccer practice.

This whole Laurel problem was so unbelievably

confusing. Dylan leaned back in his seat as he stopped at a red light. It was also starting to get on his nerves. Dylan had been nothing but patient. He'd been a good friend to Laurel, he'd hatched this ridiculous plan for her, all the while holding back from what he really wanted to do—kiss her— so that she'd know she could trust him.

And she can only think about Gavin, Dylan knew. The light turned green, and Dylan almost crashed into the silver Range Rover right in front of him, slamming his foot on the accelerator with a little too much force.

This is all so stupid, he thought, braking to create some space between his car and the SUV. *What am I supposed to do? Just sit around and wait until Laurel is ready? If* she ever was, of course.

He shook his head as he made a left turn onto Magnolia Lane. And then what about tomorrow night, at Ava's party? Was Dylan supposed to step aside as Laurel hung out with the guy she wished was her boyfriend, winning him over because of a plan that Dylan had concocted?

This is too lame, Dylan thought, driving along the curvy, downhill road. The worst part of it all was that Laurel was now so weird around him. Almost rude. Acting as if they barely knew each other.

Screw that. Dylan made a quick right onto Founders Road. He didn't have to put up with this. He didn't have to sit around and wait, acting like a fool to get Laurel's attention. Come to think of it, Dylan didn't even have to go to Ava's party tomorrow night to help Laurel out.

Yeah, Dylan thought, slowing up as he neared a stop sign. *I* won't *go.* No girl was worth *this.*

Dylan sighed, coming to a complete stop.

No girl except, of course, Laurel.

Fourteen

"I STILL CAN'T believe we're here!" Liza exclaimed, snaking her arm around Laurel's shoulders and hugging her close. There were tears shining in Liza's pretty blue eyes.

Laurel hugged Liza back, her heart bursting. "I've missed you so much," Laurel whispered.

"I can't believe how tan Laurel is when we're so pale," Gavin commented, a gleam in his dark blue eyes. He smiled—that lopsided, sweet smile that had always taken her breath away.

Laurel smiled back. She was happier than she ever realized she'd be that they were here. Even Gavin. They'd arrived a couple of hours ago. Laurel and her parents had driven to the airport to pick them up, and after a little rest at the house Liza, Laurel, and Gavin had walked the three blocks to Chummy's, a hamburger joint.

"I can't believe how warm and sunny it is here," Liza said. "Just like on television. I can't wait to go sight-seeing tomorrow, Laur."

"Me too," Laurel said with a smile. "I haven't seen much myself yet either."

Gavin ruffled his shiny brown hair. "Do you believe I have to spend the *whole* day with my aunt? I wish I could hang out with you guys." He leaned back in the seat and draped his arm along the back of the booth. The arm she used to dream was around her. "She's not springing me till it's time for your party."

Laurel tilted her head. She was surprised she was glad to hear that. Spending the day with Gavin would be difficult. She might have another guy on the brain, but her feelings for Gavin hadn't completely evaporated. Maybe they never would. She had known him too long and had cared for him too much. Plus it had been only a few weeks ago that he'd broken her heart.

"Hmmm. Then Liza and I will just have to find a way to have fun without you," Laurel joked. Liza glanced at her, and Laurel realized that Liza was as surprised as she was at how well she was handling being around Gavin. Perhaps she had Dylan more on the brain than she'd thought.

Gavin smiled that incredible smile again and threw a napkin at her. Laurel laughed. How strange was this? She'd expected to feel terrible, to be practically unable to breathe in his presence. Yet here she was, joking around.

"So, um, Geena and I broke up," Gavin said, toying with his napkin.

"Gav, I know you liked the girl," Liza said, "but, um, she wasn't exactly your type. She's not known for her *brains*."

Laurel nudged Liza in the ribs. "Be nice. You once were crazy about a dumb jock. Remember Joey Mott?"

Liza laughed. "Touché."

Laurel noticed that Gavin was staring at her. He probably thought she was letting him off the hook, unofficially acknowledging that she was over the Geena issue, over him. Was that why he'd come? Because he'd broken up with Geena? If they were still together, would he have bothered flying all the way here?

Oh, who cares! Laurel thought. She had no idea if she and Gavin would ever repair their friendship, if it would ever go back to the way it used to be. She and Gavin had been close for a long time. Maybe he'd simply been so freaked out by her confession that he hadn't known how to handle it. She'd been so wrapped up in her own feelings that she hadn't even considered how awkward it must have been for him.

Maybe Gavin didn't mean to throw his feelings for Geena in my face, Laurel thought. *Maybe he just wanted things to go back to normal. He's still guilty of insensitivity, but at least I get it now.*

"Well, the only thing Gavin's missing tomorrow is dress shopping all day!" Liza exclaimed, shooting a huge smile at Laurel. "I want to buy an amazing new dress for your party!"

Laurel shifted in her seat, suddenly very uncomfortable. She'd tell Liza the truth tomorrow, after Gavin's aunt picked him up. She hated lying to their faces. It felt terrible and made her feel lower than low.

Gavin nodded. "Dress shopping is one thing I'll definitely be glad to miss." He glanced at Laurel. "Hey, so the country club must cost a fortune. Your parents are really going all out."

Laurel smiled weakly and swallowed, twirling a strand of hair around her finger. Luckily her parents were pretty much working all weekend as usual. Gavin and Liza probably wouldn't have much opportunity to chat with them. Laurel had been lucky that the subject of the country club hadn't come up during the drive from the airport. Gavin and Liza had been so obsessed with the palm trees that they simply stared out the window with their mouths hanging open.

"I'm really excited about meeting Dylan tomorrow night," Liza said, her blue eyes twinkling. "Laurel's beach dude," she added to Gavin.

Gavin nodded. "Right."

Laurel's stomach sank to the shiny wooden floor. "Of course I'll introduce you guys to him. Though, um, we're sort of not seeing each other anymore."

Liza turned concerned eyes on Laurel. "What happened?"

Laurel darted a look at Gavin. Suddenly she felt stupid. First Gavin hadn't wanted her, now another guy hadn't either. She must look great in Gavin's eyes.

"Just didn't work out, huh?" Gavin asked. "Like me and Geena, maybe."

Laurel nodded, her eyes downcast.

"I'm gonna hit the men's room," Gavin said, standing up. He headed to the back of the restaurant.

"So what happened?" Liza asked again, her eyes full of concern.

"Remember how surprised you were when I told you he hadn't kissed me the night he asked me out?" Laurel asked.

Liza nodded.

"He didn't kiss me after our date either," Laurel explained. "I guess I was so upset about the whole thing that I didn't even want to talk about it. That's why I didn't tell you." *And because I couldn't bear to hear your voice and know I was lying to you about the party—about everything,* she added mentally.

The waiter dropped the check in the middle of the table.

"I'm so sorry," Liza said, rubbing Laurel's back. "But hey, you're gonna have a great party tomorrow night, right?"

Laurel swallowed. Enough was enough. "Liza, I—"

"So what do we owe?" Gavin asked as he walked up to the table.

Laurel clamped her mouth shut. She'd wait till later and explain everything.

They divided up the bill and threw their money on the check. Laurel was desperate for some fresh air. "Ready to go, guys?"

Liza nodded. "We're outta here."

"That really is a great tan, Bayer," Gavin commented as they slid out of their booth and headed for the door.

"Thanks." Since she'd been in California, Laurel hadn't lain out in the sun once. But she probably got plenty of sun from just walking around, eating lunch outside, and playing soccer.

As Liza stopped in front of the door to rummage in her knapsack for lip gloss, Gavin put his arm across Laurel's shoulders as they walked ahead a few steps. "I'm glad I'm here," Gavin said. "You know I wouldn't have missed your birthday no matter what. Right?"

Laurel smiled. "I know, Gavin. I really do believe that now."

He winked at her, then slid his other arm around Liza as she joined them.

"I want to be the first person to wish you a happy birthday," he said. "So happy birthday. Though I've gotta say, you would've had an amazing b-day without us. A bash at a country club, all your new friends . . ."

Laurel's face flushed. She could tell them both the truth right now, she realized. Just tell them and be done with it.

But then she glanced at Gavin and felt her heart twist. Maybe she was over the heartbreak. Maybe she was crazy about another guy now. But she still couldn't bear to let him think that she'd gone to such terrible, elaborate lengths for him. That would be beyond embarrassing.

Anyway, she had Gavin to thank for one thing: He'd introduced her to the heartbreak of being liked only as a friend.

Exactly the way Dylan liked her.

School uniforms are important because . . .
because . . .

Dylan rolled his eyes and stood up, stretching as he stared out the window at the beautiful morning. He didn't care at all about school uniforms. And if he had to take a side on the issue, he'd be against them. So then why was he spending his Saturday morning trying to come up with an argument *for* school uniforms?

Dylan sighed, kicking at his tattered old soccer ball on the floor. Because he was preparing for his stupid debate and he'd been assigned to the for-uniforms side. Dylan shook his head and sat back down. He picked up the light blue index card that he'd begun to scribble on and crumpled it up in his hand.

This was so inane. Dylan *hated* debate. It was a total waste of his time. And he had no desire to be a lawyer, like his father. When it came down to it, all Dylan wanted to do was draw or paint. That was all he really cared about.

Suddenly Dylan froze in place, his neck stiffening. Wasn't it time his father knew that already? Wasn't it time for Dylan to stop doing whatever his father ordered him to? It was, after all, *Dylan's* life.

He stomped out of his room, took the stairs two at a time, and headed straight for the den. It was time Dylan told his dad how he felt, once and for all.

But as Dylan walked into the den and saw his father sitting in the stiff, dark brown leather chair in the corner of the room, one leg crossed over the other and reading *Forbes,* his determination wavered.

At the sound of Dylan's footsteps, his dad glanced up from his magazine. "How are those debate notes coming?" he asked. "I'm ready to look at them whenever you are."

Tell him, Dylan ordered himself, both of his hands balling into fists. *You have to tell him.*

His father raised his dark eyebrows while he waited for a response. "Dylan?"

"I hate debate, Dad."

168

His father blinked. "Hate debate? You've never said that."

Dylan stuck his hands in his pockets. "I know. Because you've been telling me and telling me that debate is crucial to my getting into the right college. Crucial to my becoming a lawyer one day. But I don't *want* to be a lawyer. I don't *want* to take debate."

His dad seemed to be waiting for him to finish up, to get to some kind of point. Dylan shook his head. Why was this so difficult? Why did he have such a hard time talking to his father? He sighed and dropped down into the couch next to his father's chair.

"Dad, the debate team was okay when it didn't conflict with other stuff."

"Other stuff?"

Dylan glanced up at his father. "Painting. It conflicts with the painting class that I want to take. I only agreed to take debate because it was so important to you. I figured I'd deal with it. But now . . ."

His dad sat up straighter. "But Dylan, painting won't impress Ivy League—"

"No, Dad, just listen for a sec," Dylan interrupted. He stood up and began to pace around the room. He was not going to let his father get the last word on this one. "Painting is just as impressive an activity for applications as debate. In some ways, it's even better. Do you know how many debate-club members and class presidents those admissions officers see?"

"Well." Dylan's father's eyebrows scrunched together. "I never considered that—"

Dylan sat back down. "Dad," he interrupted. "You know what I realized? That *that* isn't even the point. The point is that I *love* to paint. And draw. And I even think I'm good at it. It might even be what I want to do with the rest of my life. So I don't see why I should take something I hate rather than something I really care about."

Stephen Fraiser crossed his arms over his chest. For a moment Dylan thought his father was going to argue. But then he simply let out a heavy sigh and said, "You've never expressed how important this was to you before."

Dylan nodded. "I know."

Why not? That was the question. What had he been so afraid of?

Getting what I want, he suddenly realized. And failing at it. The way he did with Laurel.

His father took a deep breath. "I'm not sure I love the idea of you pursuing a career that's not so secure, but if it's painting you love, then that's what you should go after. If you're looking for my permission to drop debate, you've got it."

Dylan's eyes widened. So that was what it took. To stand up and say what you wanted. "Thanks, Dad."

Dylan had always figured he *couldn't* get what

he wanted ever since he'd been told he couldn't live with his mother, country to country. He'd stopped asking for anything then. Suddenly he understood the real reason why he'd hooked up with so many girls, unable to commit. Because he'd never found one he really, really wanted, the way he wanted to paint, and to travel, and to explore. Until Laurel.

"Hey, Dylan," his father said.

Uh-oh, here we go, Dylan thought. *He's gonna add how disappointed in me he is. How I can do what I want, but he's not pleased.*

"You're a lot like your mother," his dad said, peering at him over the rims of his glasses. "We didn't see eye to eye on a lot of things either. You know that."

Dylan stared at his father, not sure what to say.

"Just because our differences drove us apart," his father continued, "doesn't mean I don't respect her. And just because you and I see things differently doesn't mean I don't love and respect you. I always will, Dylan. Always."

Dylan was stunned. His father stood, eyeing him. Dylan walked over, and his dad extended his arms. They embraced.

"I'm proud of you," his father said, dropping back down into the chair. "In fact, you've proven you definitely don't need to take debate. Look how well you convinced me to change my mind."

Dylan laughed. "I'll see you later, Dad."

His father smiled and opened his magazine.

I can't believe it, Dylan thought as he walked up the carved wooden staircase. *I can't believe I not only get to drop debate, but that I actually made major headway in my relationship with my father.*

Dylan replayed the whole conversation with his father, trying to understand how it had all been so simple. Man. He smiled as he recalled saying: *Do you know how many debate-club members and class presidents those admissions officers see?* Those words had come straight from Laurel's mouth.

Dylan sank down into his desk chair. Come to think of it, all of this—getting up the guts to confront his father, realizing it was ridiculous to take debate instead of painting—all this had been a result of Laurel's advice. He had *her* to thank.

He opened his desk drawer and pulled out his drawing of Laurel, which was nearly done. He shook his head. The girl might have caused him plenty of grief, but truth be told, she'd brought only positives to Dylan's life. And he wasn't about to give up on her. Any doubts that Dylan had about going to Ava's party had now been erased. He was going. Period.

The phone rang, interrupting his thoughts. "Hello?"

"Hi. Could I speak to Dylan, please?" an unfamiliar-sounding woman's voice asked.

"This is Dylan."

"This is Ellie Bayer, Laurel's mom? I hope I'm

not imposing, but I have a question for you."

Dylan raised his eyebrows, leaning back in his chair as Laurel's mother continued to speak.

Hmmm. Now, this sounded interesting. . . .

On Saturday afternoon Laurel was feeling better than she had in days. For one, it was her birthday! She and Liza had stayed up most of the night (Gavin slept in the guest/Dani's room downstairs), talking and giggling about old times. And then this morning Laurel's parents had created something of a birthday breakfast surprise.

Her dad had made Laurel's favorite chocolate-chip pancakes, which he and her mom had brought to the table with seventeen candles—sixteen plus one for luck—for Laurel to blow out. Everyone had sung happy birthday, and then they dug in, laughing, talking, stuffing their faces.

Laurel's parents gave her a new stereo system. Liza had given her a silver cuff bracelet, and Gavin's gift was two CDs by new bands he liked. It had been a wonderful morning. Then, after Gavin's aunt had picked him up, Liza had gone with Laurel to take her driver's test . . . and Laurel had passed! That was a major relief. Not to mention an unbelievable feeling of freedom.

And then Laurel had the pleasure of *driving* her friend to the Beverly Center—a place that Laurel hadn't been to yet herself. It was in essence a mall, except the large, airy space had much cooler stores than any shopping center near Grange ever had. In the hour they'd spent there, Liza had basically gone on a buying spree, and she'd even convinced Laurel to buy a little black dress for the party tonight. A dress that Laurel had to admit she didn't look half bad in.

Now the two friends were sitting at a table at Chin Chin's—one of Laurel's friends from the soccer team worked there and had sworn by the restaurant's nouveau-Chinese food. Laurel and Liza were sharing an overflowing Chinese chicken salad.

Laurel was relishing having Liza here in California. Relishing being in a good mood. And relishing the fact that her brain wasn't occupied with worries about the stupid party.

Until Liza brought it up, of course.

"I can't wait to meet all of your new friends tonight," Liza exclaimed, stabbing some shredded cucumber pieces with her fork.

As Laurel swallowed her piece of sesame-dressed chicken, she couldn't take it any longer. Laurel couldn't lie to Liza for one moment more.

It was time to tell her the truth.

"Tonight's party isn't mine," Laurel quickly blurted out. "It's another girl's. I was simply invited."

Liza blinked, her lips parting slightly. *"What?"*

Laurel squeezed her eyes shut, her face heating up. She was so embarrassed! After opening her eyes and taking a deep breath, Laurel told Liza everything. *Everything.*

174

How she'd lied about the party to prove something to Gavin, how she'd exaggerated about meeting a guy on the beach for Gavin's sake, and how, in the end, it turned out that Dylan wasn't even the least bit interested in her anyway.

When Laurel finally finished her long, sorry story, she cringed, holding her hands up to her eyes and dreading Liza's response. But in true Liza form, Liza was understanding and forgiving and didn't make fun of Laurel at all. Of course she was shocked, but she quickly got over that. In fact, she tried to comfort her.

Liza pushed a stray red-blond curl behind her ear. "I know exactly how you feel. Even though you sort of forgive Gavin now, I can see why you still can't tell him the truth."

Laurel nodded. "Thanks for understanding. And for not being mad at me."

Liza hugged Laurel. "Wow. So all this trouble and now it's Dylan you like! And now he thinks you're still in love with Gavin."

Laurel's shoulders slumped. "It's not like that matters anyway. He only likes me as a friend."

Liza propped her elbows onto the table and rested her chin in the palms of her hands. "Oh, Laur. I know that stinks. But, well, it's a start, isn't it? I mean, friends can lead to more sometimes. . . ."

"Yeah, for other girls," Laurel said, letting out a short, frustrated laugh. "That's all guys ever want me as—as a friend."

"Not all," Liza said. "Just Gavin and *maybe* Dylan. Who knows how either of them really feels? I mean, think about it, Laur. You told Gavin you had feelings for him a few days before you were moving halfway across the country! Maybe he figured a relationship was impossible. Maybe *that's* why he turned to Geena."

Laurel tilted her head. She'd never really thought of that. Maybe it didn't matter anymore, but it sure did make her feel better.

"And Dylan—who knows?" Liza said. "Maybe he *does* like you. Maybe you've just got to give it time."

But today's *my birthday,* Laurel thought. *What a present that would be—Dylan telling me he does like me on my sixteenth birthday, even if we're at someone else's party. Dylan dancing with me cheek to cheek.*

It was just a stupid fantasy. It would never, ever happen.

"Laur, you never know," Liza said. "Life is full of surprises."

Laurel smiled weakly, and Liza shot an arm over her shoulders. "I'm so glad you're my friend, Liza."

"Ditto," Liza said. "And hey, we'd better go. We have to get ready for your party!"

"You mean *Ava's* party," Laurel reminded her.

Liza giggled. "Let's go pull off the hoax of the century!"

Fifteen

"THIS IS TOTALLY unreal," Gavin said as he, Laurel, and Liza stood in the middle of Pasadena Valley Country Club's pool area.

Laurel nodded. Talk about unreal. Her black tank dress was suddenly feeling way too short for comfort. If only she hadn't let Liza talk her into dressing like . . . like she was the star of her own sweet sixteen. Laurel had never worn a dress like this before. It made her feel more grown up, even sexy. But what was the point?

Gavin would probably make fun of it.

And Dylan wouldn't even notice.

"Laurel, your parents really went all out," Gavin continued. "Wow."

Laurel had to agree. The place did look as incredible as Dylan had predicted. The sun had just set, casting a pink haze across the club's lush, verdant surroundings, and the pathway that led from the lobby to the pool was lined with tall candle torches. The pool was lit up, and tiny white Christmas lights were wrapped around the deck's veranda like ivy. The area was already swarming with people—Ava's guests, both young and old, dressed to the nines, were mingling, and a bunch of servers wearing white jackets, black bow ties, and black pants were walking around with silver trays.

"Yup. Your parents sure know how to throw a party," Liza commented wryly, wrapping her hot pink shawl more tightly around her black-and-pink floral dress.

Laurel gently elbowed Liza in the ribs.

Gavin tugged on the knot of his tie. "Where are they anyway? I don't see your mom and dad anywhere. I'd really like to compliment them on the party."

Laurel's stomach turned over. "Uh, probably talking to the chef, taking care of last minute plans or something." The lie sounded completely stupid to her ears. And Dylan had promised that this would be easy to explain.

Laurel bit her lip, scanning the party for him. Where *was* he anyway?

Gavin glanced all around. "Laurel, do you *know* everyone here? Who are they?"

Strangely enough, Laurel recognized a lot of the guests. She knew practically all the teenagers from Hunt, of course, and she had seen many of the adults around the school grounds, picking up or dropping off students, especially after soccer practice. Granted, there were a lot of people she'd never seen before in her life—Ava's relatives and her parents' friends, she figured. But suddenly Laurel found herself feeling a bit more comfortable.

"Um, let's see," she told Gavin. "Classmates and business associates and relatives." That wasn't a lie. These people simply weren't her relatives or her parents' business associates. But they were her classmates.

Gavin lifted his eyebrows, sticking out his thin bottom lip. "Huh. You've definitely made friends fast."

Laurel smiled. "The entire class was invited." Another truth. Just then a waitress walked over with a tray filled with food. "Crab cakes?" she offered, holding the platter in front of them.

"Cool," Gavin said, helping himself to one and popping it into his mouth. Liza took one as well, but Laurel passed. The way her nerves were duking it out in her stomach, eating was downright impossible. "I didn't even know you liked crab cakes, Laur."

Laurel smiled weakly. "I don't, but other people do, so . . ." She gripped her little black crocheted purse, which she'd borrowed from Liza. How was she going to make it through this night? Gavin had way too many questions, and Laurel had too many stupid answers.

Once again she scanned the area for Dylan. All she saw were a bunch of people she didn't know. Where the heck was he?

"So let's circulate already," Gavin went on. "I want to meet your friends."

"Yeah, okay, um—" Laurel broke off as her gaze landed on Ava. She looked gorgeous in a floor-length red dress, her long brown hair piled on top of her head. She was surrounded by people—friends from school and some of the adults. No doubt they were all wishing her happy birthday and telling her just how lovely *her* party was.

Laurel felt like such a fraud.

And now Gavin was taking a step in Ava's direction.

The back of Laurel's neck started to sweat. "Um, let's go get a drink first, though," she said quickly. Laurel pinched Liza's waist, motioning to the problem area with her eyes.

Liza glanced at Ava and nodded, immediately getting it. "Yeah. Come on, I'm thirsty."

The two girls headed toward the bar, which was in the opposite direction of Ava. Thankfully, Gavin followed. They maneuvered their way to an opening at the bar, next to a group of boisterous adults.

Gavin squeezed Laurel's shoulder, and she

glanced at him. He was looking her up and down. "You look great, Laur." He smiled, his eyes twinkling. "Really great."

Laurel stared back at him. "Thanks." So he had noticed.

She didn't know if it was because her nerves were in overdrive or because she really was one hundred percent over Gavin, but his compliment— a compliment that Laurel would have *killed* to hear a month ago—now barely registered in her brain. At least, not in *that* way.

At the moment there was only one thing on her mind.

Where was Dylan?

Dylan ran through Pasadena Valley Country Club's lobby as fast as he could, his pulse racing. He took a moment to catch his breath at the entrance to the pool area.

He'd planned to get to Ava's party early—or at least on time. But the forces of the universe seemed to be totally against him tonight. His car had broken down. Luckily it had happened right near a gas station, but he'd had to wait for a tow truck and then a cab to take him to the country club. What a bust.

He hoped everything was okay—that Laurel hadn't run into any problems. He should have been here to help her from the beginning. Now she probably hated him.

He was in a great position to tell the girl how he felt, Dylan thought grimly.

He stepped onto the deck, his stomach sinking. No one, save for a few servers who were tidying up, was out here. Dylan had missed the cocktail hour. He glanced down at his watch; he was a little under an hour late. They must have just moved all of the party goers inside.

Laurel's going to kill me, Dylan thought as he headed for the club's ballroom, his ears immediately filled with the roaring of a festive crowd. The band was already set up on the platform by the dance floor. At the moment they were playing jazz music.

I tell her this will be so easy and then I'm not even here to help her. Dylan took a couple of steps inside, his eyes darting around the room for Laurel.

Then he saw her.

He nearly collapsed onto the burgundy-and-gold carpeting.

Laurel looked amazing. He'd always thought she looked beautiful in just jeans and a T-shirt, but seeing Laurel in a body-hugging black dress—a dress that emphasized her tiny waist, her unbelievable curves . . . well, she absolutely took his breath away.

She was standing in the far corner of the room, sipping water from a wineglass, and for a moment Dylan just froze, watching her. His knees felt weak as he took in Laurel's thick, glossy hair, her radiant, shimmering eyes, the toned curves of her legs. . . .

He shook his head, forcing himself to snap out of it. *Stop staring, idiot,* he thought. *Go over there and help her with this mess already.*

Dylan walked toward Laurel, weaving his way around the crowds, ignoring whoever was calling his name, never taking his eyes off her. She was standing next to a cute girl with long, curly hair who Dylan figured was Liza.

A tall, lanky, good-looking guy stood on Laurel's other side. A bitter taste came to Dylan's mouth as the guy casually draped his arm around Laurel's slim shoulders, giving her a squeeze. The way that guy was touching Laurel with such a look of ownership, he had to be Gavin.

The guy she'd gone to all this trouble for.

The enemy.

Dylan put on his best and brightest smile. "Hey. Sorry I'm so late!" He walked up to Laurel and her two friends. "Laurel, happy birthday!"

Laurel's dark eyes widened, her face tensing. "Thanks, Dylan," she said, her tone flat. "Glad you could make it."

Dylan smiled weakly and nodded. *Man.* She was even angrier than he expected. That was a surprise. He'd expected her to be *so* happy that the famous Gavin was here that she'd barely notice anything else. She must be really worried about pulling off the scam. That Gavin might discover the truth.

"Sorry I'm late," Dylan repeated. "Car trouble—" He cut himself off as he realized that his excuse was getting no reaction from Laurel. She was just standing there, tapping her unpolished nail against the rim of her glass, her expression blank. He shook his head. "Anyway. Doesn't matter." He turned to Liza, holding out a hand. "You must be Liza. Heard a lot about you."

"Heard a lot about you too," Liza said, shaking his hand. He noticed a twinkling gleam in her eyes. The girl had obviously been let in on the truth.

He turned to Gavin, clearing his throat. "Hey. I'm Dylan."

Gavin shook his hand too. Dylan had been in the guy's presence for two seconds and already he hated him. Hated the way he was touching Laurel, especially after he had so obviously broken her heart.

"Hi, everyone! We're finally here!"

Dylan turned around to see Cara in a long, black skirt and silver wrap top next to a very annoyed-looking Dave.

"Did we miss much?" she asked "Dave got lost."

Dave rolled his eyes. "I *did not* get lost. *You* were a bad navigator."

Cara laughed and turned her attention to Liza and Gavin. "How's it going? You must be Laurel's friends from home. . . . Oh—Laurel—happy birthday!"

"Thanks," Laurel said, eyeing Cara. "How'd you—"

Laurel shot him a questioning glance. He had a feeling Laurel had just stopped herself from asking Cara how she knew it was Laurel's birthday. *That* would have been a disaster.

He glanced around the room. He spotted plenty of potential other disasters. A few feet away, Ava stood near the dance floor, surrounded by people and looking like this was her party. Laurel's friends definitely couldn't meet *her* tonight.

Then Dylan noticed Ava's father, talking with some friends by the bar area. *What if Ava's dad decides to make some sort of speech?* he wondered, his neck tensing. Come to think of it, there was no way he wouldn't. The guy was a total ham. Dylan clenched his teeth, turning back to his friends. *Why* had he thought this would be so easy?

Jenny Meyer passed by, then backed up in front of Laurel. "Hey," she said. "Isn't it your birthday today?"

Gavin, who had finally removed his arm from Laurel's shoulders, scrunched his eyebrows together, looking confused. "Of course it is. It's—"

"Can you show me where the bathrooms are?" Liza quickly broke in, hooking her arm through Jenny's and leading her away.

Dylan let out a deep breath, surprised by the close call. It was a good thing Laurel had told Liza the truth. They needed all the help they could get.

"Something is up tonight," Dave said. "People are acting *weird*."

Laurel shot Dylan a look, and he glanced down, scratching the back of his neck. *Man.* Tonight was going to be a very long night.

"Laur?" Gavin said. "How about a walk outside for a sec? I'd like to talk to you about something." He draped his arm around her shoulders again.

The name's Laurel, Dylan wanted to yell. *And get your arm off her.*

Say no, he mentally commanded, staring at Laurel as if he could relay his message through his eyes. *Say no. Don't go off with him. He hurt you. He's a jerk. He lives most of the way across the country. Forget him.*

But Laurel didn't even glance Dylan's way. "Okay."

Gavin took her hand. "Nice meeting you," Gavin said to Dylan and Dave as he led Laurel off toward the door.

She glanced over her shoulder. "See you guys later."

Was that a smile he saw on her lips? he wondered nervously. Was she letting him know that this might be the big moment? The moment Gavin told her he was sorry, that he'd made a mistake?

Dylan simply stood there, feeling like a fool, watching Laurel walk away with the jerk. And he was powerless to do anything.

Dave crossed his arms over his chest. "That's the guy from Ohio?"

Dylan nodded, watching the two of them weave around the crowds, circling around a waiter carrying a tray.

"He's really into her," Dave commented. "It's obvious."

Dylan nodded again, watching Gavin lead Laurel to the door. "Yeah. I know."

"Well?" Dave prodded. "What are you going to do about it?"

Dylan's shoulders slumped. They were out the door.

He sighed. "Nothing."

Dave gawked at him. "Nothing?"

"What can I do?" Dylan asked. "This is what she wants."

Dave looked at him. "Says who?"

"Says her."

"I thought she was getting *over* him," Dave pointed out. "That doesn't mean she *still* wants him."

But why would she go to all this trouble . . . ?

Suddenly Dylan understood. It was sort of like the reason he had been unable to tell his father the truth about what he wanted: *fear.* Fear of different things, maybe, but fear nonetheless. Laurel was afraid for Gavin to know that she wasn't having some big shindig. That she hadn't made two hundred best friends in two weeks.

Maybe Dylan did have a chance.

Maybe.

Sixteen

LAUREL DIDN'T KNOW why she had agreed to come outside with Gavin.

She didn't mind the break, that was for sure. As long as they were out here together, Gavin wouldn't have a million questions. And Laurel wouldn't have to hide things from him. Pretending took a lot out of a person.

Plus she was so upset with Dylan! Okay, he had car trouble. But still. This whole charade was his brilliant idea, and he'd been late to help her out. She definitely needed a moment away from him.

Especially because the sight of him had taken her breath away. He wore black pants and a black jacket. With his blond hair and green eyes, all that black made him look so mysterious, so amazing, so gorgeous. . . .

She noticed Gavin fidgeting. She stopped thinking about Dylan and turned her attention to Gavin. He seemed nervous about something. He kept kicking at the edge of the pool deck, where the slate met the manicured grass, both hands digging deep in his pockets.

She took the moment to look up at the starfilled night sky. She made a wish. A wish she doubted would ever come true.

A wish about Dylan.

"Gavin?" she said. "Did you want to talk to me?"

"Okay, okay, here's the thing," Gavin suddenly burst out, finally looking at her. "Remember, um, what you told me before you left Grange? About, um, how you felt . . . about me?"

A flush rose up in Laurel's cheeks. Her grasp on her little black purse tightened. "Yes." As if she'd ever forget.

Gavin nodded, shifting his weight from one foot to the other. "Okay," he repeated.

And then, before Laurel even had a chance to realize what was happening, Gavin jumped forward and moved in. And started kissing her.

"Whoa. *Whoa*," Laurel said, pushing away immediately, her brain reeling. "What's *that*?"

"What?" Gavin blinked, his blue eyes wide. "You told me you liked me as more than a friend, and I've been feeling that way ever since I got here yesterday, so I figured I would—"

"Make out with me?" Laurel supplied.

Gavin glanced down at the ground, then back up at Laurel. "It seemed appropriate, I guess. Just *showing* you how I feel."

Laurel was stunned. She had no interest in kissing Gavin. None at all.

"Gavin," she began. "I meant everything I said to you before I left Grange. But I don't . . . feel that way anymore. I'm sorry. . . ."

Gavin nodded, still looking down. "Oh."

"No, listen. I still love you . . . as a friend." Gavin glanced up. "And you know what? I don't think you really like me that way either. I think you miss hanging out with me, and you broke up with Geena, and I'm all dressed up tonight, so . . ."

Gavin gave her a weak smile. "You must think I'm a total jerk."

"No. I don't." Laurel felt a lightness in her heart as she realized she really meant it. She no longer held any anger toward Gavin. She was over him and still wanted him to be her friend.

And as Laurel let out a deep breath and stared back at Gavin, noticing how uncomfortable he seemed, she decided that she was going to tell him the truth.

It was time. She didn't want to lie anymore. Nor did she have to. If she and Gavin were ever going to be friends again, real friends, he deserved the truth. And she deserved to feel embarrassed while telling it.

"Gavin, I have to tell you something."

He raised his eyebrows.

Oh, boy. Laurel bit her lip. Here went nothing. Now Gavin would see who the real jerk was.

Right now, Dylan knew, Laurel and Gavin were in the process of getting together. Becoming the couple she'd dreamed of them becoming.

And he also figured he had no shot with her whatsoever. But he didn't care.

After a few moments of tense hesitation, standing frozen in place, Dylan decided that he liked Laurel way too much to just stand back and do nothing. He wasn't going to give up without a fight.

Not give up without a fight? Since when did I become the leading actor in one of those cheesy romantic comedies? Dylan wondered as he navigated his way around boogying people on the dance floor.

Whatever, Dylan thought, pushing through the door that led to the deck. It didn't matter. All that mattered was that he told Laurel how he felt, once and for all. After that, it was up to her. All he knew was that he was no longer afraid to ask for what he wanted.

And what he wanted was for Laurel to be his girlfriend.

Dylan immediately spotted them. He swallowed, nervously cracking his knuckles. They were sitting on the edge of the pool deck at the far end, underneath one of the tall lampposts, their heads tipped toward each other, and they appeared to be in the middle of an intense conversation.

Just go over there anyway, Dylan told himself, watching as the breeze blew Laurel's satiny hair away from her face. *Go over there and tell her how you feel.*

Taking a deep breath, Dylan cut across the lawn and walked straight toward them.

Laurel glanced up. "Dylan?"

He gazed at her, unable to speak. For the first time in his life, he was tongue-tied. *What if she doesn't want me?* he wondered. *What if they're together?*

They both stood. Gavin stuffed his hands into his pockets and eyed him. Laurel seemed concerned. "Did you want to talk to me?" she asked.

Just say it. Say it already. Why are you wimping out? "Yes. But alone," he blurted out, before he lost his nerve. He turned to Gavin, ready to argue, ready to tell the guy that he better just give him a moment with Laurel.

Even if he'd already lost her.

But Gavin didn't protest. He smiled, actually. "I'm going to go find Liza. See you later, Laur. Later, Dylan."

"Later," Dylan repeated blankly. He watched the guy amble away, then turned to face Laurel.

"Dylan?" she said. "What's going on?"

He gazed into Laurel's gorgeous chocolate brown eyes. He opened his mouth, ready to tell her just how he felt about her. But he was interrupted by a blaring soft-rock ballad floating out from the ballroom. Gavin hadn't closed the door when he'd gone back in.

Wonderful. Now he even had the cheesy background music to go with this whole stuck-in-a-romantic-comedy scenario.

"I don't know what just went on between you and Gavin," Dylan began. "And I don't know how you feel about me . . ." Pause. Glance down. Glance back up. "But I want you to know I like you a lot."

There. Dylan held his breath, his neck muscles tightening. He'd said it.

Dylan had preimagined all of Laurel's possible negative reactions to his declaration—that she'd laugh or immediately tell him she wasn't interested. But at the moment, after absorbing Dylan's words, Laurel did something completely unexpected: She rolled her eyes.

"Right. I know." Laurel jiggled the silver cuff bracelet around her wrist. "As a friend."

What? What the heck was she talking about? "No, Laurel. I mean, I *like* you. Not as a friend. I mean, yes, as a friend, but more. Much, much more."

Laurel narrowed her eyes at him.

"I want you to be my girlfriend," he said.

Laurel's mouth dropped open. "But . . . I—" She glanced down, then back up at him. "I don't understand. I—why didn't you let me know? Why didn't you . . . kiss me? Not even once?"

Dylan was shocked. She was doubting him because he *hadn't* tried to hook up with her? This was insane! "I've never kissed you because I didn't want you to get the wrong idea."

"Right." Laurel nodded. "You didn't want me to think that you liked me."

"No," Dylan corrected, shaking his head. "I didn't want you to think I liked you only as a *hookup."* He sighed. This had to be the most ridiculous conversation in the history of conversations. "Look, maybe you don't even know this about me . . . but I kinda have a reputation. As a player."

Laurel gnawed her lower lip. Meanwhile Dylan's stomach twisted and turned. *Great,* he thought. *Good going, Dyl. You had to remind her that you've hooked up with half the junior class at Hunt.*

"No," Laurel said slowly, her eyes searching Dylan's face. "It doesn't make sense. If you really liked me, then why—I mean, how come . . ." Laurel let out a short, breathy sigh, her voice drifting off, as if she didn't know how to explain what she wanted to say.

But suddenly Dylan realized exactly how to express what he wanted to say. "Okay, you want proof?" He unbuttoned his blazer, reaching into his inside pocket. "Here," he said, unfolding the thick piece of paper. "I started this the day I met you."

Laurel's eyes widened as she took the drawing. The drawing of her beautiful face. She let out a small gasp. "Oh, Dylan," she whispered. "Wow." She stared from the drawing to him and back again.

Dylan smiled, relief flooding through him.

It was enough. He knew he had her.

Laurel gazed down at the drawing of herself, feeling the world swirl around her, feeling the earth give underneath her strappy sandals. Dylan had said he'd started this the day he'd met her. . . .

Laurel took in a deep breath, warmth rushing through her body, tears coming to her eyes. It just seemed too incredibly good to be true.

"*Now* do you believe me?" Dylan asked gently.

Laurel glanced up and looked right into Dylan's amazing green eyes. He was smiling, that cleft in his chin deepening, his eyes holding more meaning than ever. Laurel's pulse quickened as she realized that *that* look, that gaze she'd always felt had to mean something, actually did.

Dylan felt the same way about her as she did about him.

"And all along I've liked *you*," Laurel whispered,

her limbs feeling shaky. "All along I've wanted to . . . ."

"Do this?" Dylan asked, stepping closer and cupping Laurel's chin in his rough hand.

Goose bumps popped out on every inch of Laurel's skin as Dylan gently brushed her hair behind her ears. Tingles shot from the top of her head to the ends of her toes.

And then Dylan kissed her.

Laurel closed her eyes and kissed him back.

Her senses went into overdrive. She knew that she'd never forget the clean smell of Dylan's soap, the hint of spicy aftershave scent, the feel of his surprisingly soft cheek, the way the breeze was whipping through her hair, or the taste of his gentle lips. . . .

She'd never forget *anything* about her first kiss with Dylan.

Including the sound of the bandleader calling the party to attention and announcing, "Ladies and gentlemen, it's time to cut the cake. Please join us in singing 'Happy Birthday' to Ava."

Laurel pulled slightly apart from Dylan, giggling. "I thought they never did stuff like that here. That it was too 'tacky' for this place."

Dylan laughed. "So maybe they're more down-to-earth than I thought. Who knew singing 'Happy Birthday' was still in style at the Pasadena Valley Country Club?"

"Good thing I told my friends the truth," she murmured.

197

Dylan nodded, gazing into her eyes. "I was so worried."

She stood up on her tiptoes and kissed him, a gentle kiss on his soft lips. "It was always you, Dylan. From the moment I saw you at lunch. It was you."

He smiled, and she thought he was about to lean down and kiss her again. But he stood up straight, as if suddenly remembering something. He reached into his jacket pocket and pulled out yet another thick piece of paper.

"Here," he said. "I almost forgot."

Laurel took the cream-colored paper in her hands. Her body felt like Jell-O—her *brain* felt like Jell-O—from the kiss and all that had happened tonight. She took a deep breath and read what was beautifully printed in purple ink:

Your presence is requested
at your very own sweet-sixteen bonfire.
Tomorrow night, seven o'clock.
Casual attire.

"What . . . what does this mean?" Laurel asked, confused.

He placed a hand on each of Laurel's almost bare shoulders, causing shivers to run up and down her spine. "Your mom called and told me she wanted to plan something for you. I said you mentioned you'd really love a bonfire on the beach."

Laurel's heart pounded, her grip tightening on the card. She thought of her mom, then her dad, then her two sisters. This was, without a doubt, one of the sweetest things anyone had done for her.

"Dylan, that's so—" She shook her head, at a loss for words.

Dylan squeezed her shoulders, smiling. "It's gonna be tomorrow night since Liza and Gavin'll still be here. Cara and Dave are coming. And some surprise guests too."

"Wow," Laurel whispered, overcome with emotion. She felt like she was in a wonderful dream. All her birthday wishes had come true.

Including Dylan as her fantasy date for her sweet sixteen.

But it wasn't a fantasy. It was real.

Laurel bit her lip, staring into Dylan's eyes. "I don't know what to say. . . . I don't know what to—"

"You don't need to say anything," Dylan told her, stroking her hair. And then, as the party goers wound down their rendition of "Happy Birthday," Dylan leaned down to kiss Laurel again.

But before his lips met hers, he whispered, "Happy sweet sixteen."

Is He Your Perfect Sweet-Sixteen Sweetie?

Whether your sweet-sixteen party is a lavish affair at a country club (like Ava's), a small, intimate gathering in your house, or just you and your best bud (or crush!) hanging out, you've probably been dreaming of your sixteenth birthday for months. Will your guy appreciate the importance of the big day? Take our special quiz to find out!

1. *After baby-sitting all afternoon, you run into your guy at the pizza shop. He:*

A. ignores his friends and hangs out with you instead

B. invites you to join him and his friends

C. asks if that's baby spit on your shoulder and walks away

2. *You have to pull an all-nighter to finish the term paper due tomorrow. He:*

A. offers to help with research

B. offers moral support and a hazelnut coffee

C. offers to keep you company until he finishes his own homework

3. *He calls you to talk about:*

A. the mean thing your kid brother said

B. how your doctor appointment went

C. himself

4. *In his spare time he:*

A. writes songs about you

B. thinks up fun things to do with you

C. works out and tries out new hairstyles

5. *Your new haircut is, um, a little short. He:*

    A. cuts his own hair to match

    B. says you're beautiful

    C. hands you his baseball cap

6. *His prized possession is:*

A. a picture of your family pet

B. a picture of you

C. a picture of himself

7. *When selecting a video, your guy:*

    A. has no opinion

    B. chooses one you'll both like

    C. insists on a slice and dice

8. You accidentally belch in his presence. He:

A. belches too

B. laughs

C. tells everyone

9. When you tell him your sweet-sixteen dress is lavender, he:

A. offers to wear a lavender suit

B. asks what color you'd like your corsage to be

C. makes a face

10. You knew he really wanted to be your sweet-sixteen date when he:

A. got down on his hands and knees and begged

B. asked you

C. took it for granted

So is he your perfect sweet-sixteen sweetie?

If you circled mostly A's:

The good news is that this guy will probably appreciate pretty much *anything* you do. But as you might have already guessed, this is also the bad news. While endless appreciation is always welcome from, say, a house pet, it can get somewhat tiresome from a date!

If you circled mostly B's:

Congratulations! You've found yourself a perfect sweet-sixteen sweetie. He's kind and considerate and knows how to have fun. Enjoy!

If you circled mostly C's:

This guy's too in love with himself to even remember it's your birthday! But don't worry. Turning sweet sixteen means making a birthday wish for the guy of your dreams. You'll find him.

Do you ever wonder about falling in love? About members of the opposite sex? Do you need a little friendly advice but have no one to turn to? Well, that's where we come in . . . Jenny and Jake. Send us those questions you're dying to ask, and we'll give you the straight scoop on life and love.

DEAR JAKE

Q: *I'm thirteen and my parents won't let me date. It's not fair! I really like this guy, and I think he likes me. But I can't do anything about it, unless I sneak around. If I get caught, I'll get grounded for, like, a year. What am I supposed to do?*

RS, Dallas, TX

A: You definitely don't want to be grounded for a year, so forget sneaking around. That's a good way to lose your parents' trust, instead of to gain it, which is what you want to accomplish. That's when they'll feel you're ready to date. So, in the meantime, how about telling your parents that you really like this guy, and that you'd like to invite him over to watch television or a video or for dinner. Perhaps if they're around during his visits, they'll get used to the idea of you two dating.

Q: *What do guys think about? My friend says they only think about sex and sports. Is that really true?*

PD, Jamestown, NY

A: Nope. Guys do think about girls and sports, don't get me wrong, but they also think about a lot of other things. Such as how to ask out girls they like, or what to say, or what to wear, or how to act. Surprised? Guys worry about that kind of stuff too!

Q: *My best friend, Lora, started hanging out with another girl, and now the two of them are always together. Lora's too busy to do stuff with me, and she doesn't invite me along when she has plans with her new friend. I'm really hurt. What should I do?*

PK, Topeka, KS

A: I suggest talking to Lora about how you

feel. Tell it to her straight: that you miss her and her friendship. Sometimes people get really into something new and forget the old faifthfuls—but not for long.

Q: *I'm crazy about a guy in my math class, but he doesn't even know I exist. How am I supposed to get his attention?*

MO, Springfield, IN

A: The best way to get someone's attention is by striking up a conversation. Ask him how he did on the last exam, or if you can borrow his notes from yesterday's class. Maybe he'll invite you to study with him!

DEAR JENNY

Q: *I'm totally crushed. My boyfriend started making fun of me in front of his friends, and when I got upset, he told me he was just kidding. He really made me look stupid. Is he a jerk?*

TP, Flint, Michigan

A: Sometimes guys like to show off in front of their friends. It doesn't mean that your boyfriend doesn't care about you. I suggest letting him know how much he hurt you. If he laughs it off or tells you you're too sensitive, you might have to cut him to the curb. And if he does it again, definitely dump him.

Q: *My younger sister won't leave me alone. She's always following me around and trying to hang out with me and my friends. She's a total nerd and a pain. When I complain to my parents, they tell me to be nice to her. But I don't want to be. How do I get rid of her?*

AC, Fredonia, NY

A: Well, unfortunately you're stuck with her for life. I think the best way to get rid of a pesky younger sibling is to tell her how you feel—nicely. If you make her feel like a confidante, she'll feel important, and she may stop following you around. She'll know that you'll come to her when you want to.

Q: *A friend of mine is copying everything I do. I buy a shirt at the mall—she buys the same one. I get* *bangs—she gets bangs. She's totally obvious about it. And every time she copies me, I feel like I have to change to something new. But then she copies that too! How can I get her to stop?*

KT, Buffalo, NY

A: You know what they say about imitation, right? That it's the sincerest form of flattery. But I also know how annoying it is to have someone copy you. Perhaps you can tell her that you really liked her style—before she started copying yours. She just might go back to being herself.

Q: *I'm a guy, and I hate school. Why do I have to take all these stupid classes? How am I gonna use math in the real world? School is so boring! I wish I could just go to the movies all day long.*

LJ, Tacoma, WA

A: School and the movies have a lot in common, actually. Everything you see all day long in school is sort of like watching a film: you don't know what's going to happen next, and the screen is always changing as you move from hall to hall, from class to class. And, how could learning be boring? There's nothing more exciting than learning new things, understanding new concepts, and getting smarter and smarter with every passing day and new experience! Trust me, you will need math in the real world. Otherwise, how would you know if the clerk at the movie theater gave you the wrong change for your ticket?

Do you have any questions about love?
Although we can't respond individually to your letters,
you just might find your questions answered in our column.

Write to:
Jenny Burgess or Jake Korman
c/o 17th Street Productions,
an Alloy Online, Inc. company.
33 West 17th Street
New York, NY 10011

Don't miss any of the books in *Love Stories*
—the romantic series from Bantam Books!